THE IMMOLATION GAME: PHASE TWO

PENANCE TASK

MITCHELL TIERNEY

Also By Mitchell Tierney

The Immolation Game Series
The Immolation Game

Young Adult Fiction
Heather Cassidy and the Magnificent Mr Harlow

The Skellington Key

The Wandmaker's Apprentice Series
The Wandmaker's Apprentice

Everdark Realms Series
with Sabrina RG Raven
The Darkening
The Awakening

Adult Fiction
Children of the Locomotive

THE IMMOLATION GAME: PHASE TWO

THE PENANCE TASK

MITCHELL TIERNEY

The Immolation Game: Phase 02
The Penance Task

Published by Ouroborus Book Services
www.ouroborusbooks.com

Cover Design by Sabrina RG Raven
www.sabrinargraven.com

Chapter One: Slow and Quiet

Clank!

Delphi sat bolt upright. She sucked in a deep breath of cold air and looked around in a frightened panic. *Where am I?* she thought. It was somewhat familiar, but still foreign. She swung her legs off the hard, concrete bed and stood up. The metal floor sent chills through her bare feet.

'Hello?' she said, hearing her voice echo out of the room and down the hallway.

She stood for a moment, trying to remember how she had gotten there. A thought, or a memory, crossed her vision. Something that drifted into her mind's eye and quickly evaporated. She shook her head from side to side and walked carefully out and into the hallway. Voices came, soft and panicked from several feet away. She walked down the thin corridor and found a large room, painted white and void of furniture.

Three people stood talking, then suddenly stopped, and turned to Delphi.

'Who are you?'

Delphi instinctively checked her pockets, but she didn't know why. She pulled out a thin length of paper. On it was written Delphinium.

'I'm Delphinium,' she said, feeling like it wasn't for the first time. It felt like déjà vu.

A man wearing a red jumpsuit stared at her, as if he were trying to figure out where he knew her from.

'Have we met?'

'I don't think so,' Delphi responded, looking past the trio and out through the front door.

'What did you pull out of your pocket?' a woman said. She marched over to Delphi and snatched it from her hand.

'Delphinium? What does that mean? It doesn't sound like a name.'

'No, but it sounds familiar. Delphi. That's what I like to be called,' she reminisced.

The woman scrambled into her pockets and retrieved a gnarled piece of paper. She unravelled it; Latrodectus Hasseiti.

'What does it mean?'

The man looked away from them. 'Does it matter? We're here now. Must be something in the air making our memory lapse.'

'How do you know that?' a teenage girl quietly whispered.

'Well,' the man said, 'I don't have a head injury. I'm not bleeding from anywhere. We all appear healthy. It's got to be a gas leak or something? It's the only thing…'

'Can you hear that?' Delphi said, spinning around on the balls of her feet.

It was soft rustling, like shaking leaves. Latrodectus Hasseiti, still holding her piece of paper, spun around.

'It's moving… towards us.'

Delphi took a step back. The sound of gyrating floorboards, and hissing came from deep within the house. Above her she heard the familiar drop of a ball. It rolled to her right, dropped down into the wall cavity, and appeared to travel under them. The teenage girl suddenly screamed. Delphi snapped her head back around to see hundreds of small black spiders emerge from the corridor.

'Run!'

Delphi bolted. Her legs stretching in front of her body. It felt natural. Her muscles strained and felt tight. The end of the hallway opened up to a large grass field, tall and overgrown. There was a small, two foot drop down into the grass. Delphi leapt out of the hallway and landed on the lawn. The ground was soft, and the others followed. Hasseiti was behind her. She could hear her breath pounding in and out of her lungs. The teenage girl leapt high in the air and landed near her, rolling onto her knees. Her head disappeared under the long grass. The man, hesitating at the exit, was suddenly consumed with the small black spiders. They ran up his legs and across the flanking walls, leaping onto his face and shoulders. He screamed, flailing his arms around wildly before falling from the lip. Delphi ran back towards him as the spiders leapt off him and back towards the open door. She started to swat them off with her open palm, squashing them against the ground. They burst like rotten fruit, squirting black pus over his jumpsuit.

'Come on, get up,' she yelped, pulling at his sleeve. 'Run!'

The man got to his feet and started to bolt. Welts were forming over his face and neck. The woman was already in front of him, watching everything happen. Delphi turned around to find the young girl on her hands and knees, crawling through the thicket. She ran to her.

'Are you hurt?'

'No, I don't think so. My knees just gave way when I…' She lifted her left pant leg up to reveal a prosthetic leg. Her mouth fell open. 'What… I'm missing my leg?'

Delphi grabbed her and shook her by the shoulders. 'Listen, we have to get away from that door in case something else comes out. We can figure this out when...'

The man started to holler from behind the grassy field. 'I've found help! This way!'

Both girls stood up. The teenage girl ran, as if she had spent her whole life with the prosthetic. They reached the other two standing on a rocky outcropping. He was pointing down to a small town in a gully. It was surround by steep hills and forest.

'There. Someone there will know what's happening.'

'Wait,' Delphi said. 'Something isn't right. Can't you feel it?'

Hasseiti opened her mouth to argue, but then closed it

again. She could feel it too.

'Check your pockets,' she said.

'What?'

'We all had a note, something written.'

The man reached into his pockets. His hands swollen with spider venom.

'Lycosidae?' he read, looking confused.

'Phoneutria Fera,' the teenage girl said. 'Fera,' she repeated, looking at Delphi.

'Lyco,' the man said giving a satisfactory nod. He bent over frontways as the bites on his stomach started to swell. 'I don't feel great. I might need something for these bites.'

'There might be medicine down there, or antiseptic wipes,' Hasse said, looking to Delphi for agreement. She felt slightly sheepish for leaving everyone behind as she ran away.

'Okay,' Delphi concurred. 'We'll go down together and go slow and quiet.'

Fera looked at Lyco, 'Are you okay to walk?'

'They itch and sting a little, but it's okay. As long as they don't get worse.'

As they walked, Delphi looked up into the sky and could see clouds gently edging away from the sun. They were headed for some far away mountain tops. She glanced over her shoulder to see where they had come from, and all she could see was a grey shipping container with a door. To the side, it appeared to go down into the ground, where vines and weeds grew along its exterior walls. As she turned back, she could see Hasse and Lyco walking ahead of her and Fera. The young girl stood and waited for Delphi by a large boulder. There were a set of stairs carved into the dirt and rock that led down to the village. The girl had shoulder length red hair and covered her eyes from the sun. She would have been no older than sixteen.

'Do you feel like things are familiar, but also strange?' Fera said.

'It's a feeling like I've done this before, but everything is new at the same time.'

‘Do you think we all have amnesia or something? Like a medical condition?’

‘Even that question seems familiar. From what my instincts are telling me, it’s a task of some sort. I heard a loud clanking noise. It woke me up. I felt like I had to run somewhere, but I didn’t know where.’

Fera stopped suddenly. She looked down at the other two, they were talking but she couldn’t make out what they were saying. She turned her back to them nonetheless and reached into her pocket. She pulled out a silver ball the size of an egg.

‘When I woke, this popped out of a hole above my bed. I managed to grab it before it went down a hole in the floor. I think the spiders were my fault.’

Delphi felt her gut drop when she saw the metal sphere. ‘Why do you think that?’

‘Maybe the ball was meant to go down the hole?’

Delphi wanted to reach out and take it. Something inside her told her it was a commodity.

‘Maybe? If you let it go down the hole, something worse could have happened?’

Fera slipped it back in her pocket and looked towards the others, but there was no sign of them.

Chapter Two: Someone Said a Name

Hasse and Lyco had reached level ground after nearly an hour of traversing the rocky mountainside. Sweat beaded around Lyco's brow, stinging his wounds. He had started to feel dizzy, but thought it was lack of water. Lyco and Hasse both glanced around, seeing Delphi and Fera trying to catch up.

'I don't think it was such a good idea to break up the party,' Hasse said, still eyeing the two girls. Lyco looked at her, then up at the hill.

'Why? They're coming down. They probably got stuck talking or something.'

'I just don't like this place. We all seem to have the same thing happening. We should stay together.'

There was a dirt road to their left which, after a few hundred meters, turned into a gravel road and finally asphalt.

'I think they're scheming.'

Lyco's vision was blurry. He shook his head. Scratching his arms, he looked down to see he had scratched the bulbus bites so much they had started to draw blood.

'I'm sure they aren't scheming. They're probably planning to get out, like we are, or trying to figure this thing out. There's probably a reasonable excuse for all of this…'

Suddenly, everything in his vision turned to a dark tunnel. The world in front of him did a cartwheel and he lost his balance and stumbled.

'Lyco!' Hasse yelped, catching him before he fell onto the ground.

He was too heavy for her to hold, but she was able to break his fall. Gently, she lowered his to head to the ground where he leant on one knee. Delphi and Fera ran the last few steps, seeing the whole event take place. They sprinted over to him.

'It's okay,' Lyco said, holding his head. 'I just need water and to get out of this sun. I've been feeling a bit dizzy since the bites.'

Delphi looked toward the town. It was too far away to yell for help. They got Lyco to his feet and walked with him. Their steps were slow and steady. Every fifty feet they stopped and rested. Fera felt his forehead.

'He's burning up.'

'Could be exposure to the sun?'

'We'll get him to one of these houses, as quick as we can.'

Lyco blinked and saw a swimming pool. He shook his head and the vision disappeared. He closed them again and concentrated. When he opened them, he was at a party, with friends. They were cooking food on a barbeque and talking. There was music, but he didn't know who was singing. He wasn't wearing a jumpsuit, but shorts and sandals. Someone said his name.

'What did you call me?' he said, his eyes glazed over.

Delphi looked down at him. 'No one spoke to you Lyco, we're nearly there.'

'Someone said a name. My name. What was it?'

'No one said a name, Lyco,' Fera concurred with Delphi.

Hasse looked at him, worried. They left the rocky escarpment and finally got onto the asphalt road. The town stood before them. A single wide road split the shops and houses down the middle. From what they could see, there was a general store, a post office, a florist, and a chemist towards the middle. Scattered among the stores were single level houses with terracotta tiled roofs and red brick stacked chimneys. White picket fences lined the footpaths and well-manicured lawns lay identical in front of each house.

'We'll put him in the nearest house, see if anyone is there to help. While you do that, I'll run to the chemist and see what I can get,' Delphi instructed.

No one agreed or disagreed.

They approached the first house. It was a clone house of all the others. Nothing stood out except the closer they got, they could see the lush green grass was dying and the overgrown flower beds were now crowded. The house was painted cream, with a light baby-blue door. Delphi ran up to the door and banged her fist loudly on it.

'Hello!' she yelled. 'Anyone home! We need help here.' There was no answer. She peered in through the window. There was no movement either. She tried the door handle and it opened.

Delphi stepped inside. 'Hello?' she yelped again. She saw a luscious lounge near a fireplace and turned to the others. 'Bring him in here, we'll put him on the couch.'

'Is anyone there?' Fera asked, helping Hasse carry Lyco up the front porch steps.

'No one I can see,' she replied. 'I'll check next door.'

Once Delphi helped Lyco plonk down on the couch with a grunt, she rushed outside and down the front steps, heading to the house next door. It was nearly equal in colour, but it had a light pink door. She rattled her knuckles across the wood.

'Hello! Anyone home?' There was no answer. She tried another two times and peered in through the window. There was no evidence that anyone had lived in it. She took a step back and apprehensively turned the door handle. It swung open. She stared inside for a moment before going in. The floor was polished wood with Egyptian looking rugs. On the wall was a painting of horses in a field. She stopped to look at some glass vases on the mantle before heading to the kitchen. The marble countertop was granite with swirls of pale grey. She opened the fridge, but it was empty and warm. She checked the cupboard. There was two cans of pickled vegetables and a bottle of water. She grabbed them both and ran back to the first house. As she entered the house, she saw Lyco unconscious on the couch. A bottle of water was beside him, half empty.

'We found it in the cupboard, with two cans of food.'

'It's the same in the next-door house.'

'He won't wake up,' Hasse said, a quiver broke in her voice.

'I'll go down to the chemist now,' Delphi said, turning back towards the door.

'I'm coming,' Fera said, running after her.

'Best if you stay here,' Delphi protested as she took the balcony stairs two at a time.

'Hasse is there, she can watch him.'

Delphi didn't feel like protesting, so she let her follow her. They ran down the middle of the street, eyeing all the houses as they went. They were all identically built with slightly different colourations. Some were cream, while others were egg white and beige. The doors all matched their next-door neighbour's house colour. They ran past the general store, not stopping to check for supplies. When they got to the chemist, Delphi didn't hesitate to push on the door immediately, but it was locked. She tried to yank it open, but it wouldn't budge. Fera pushed her face against the glass and peered inside.

'I can see medicine on the shelves.'

'We'll have to break the glass.'

Fera stepped back and looked at Delphi, basking in her enthusiasm. Delphi ran to the centre of the road where there was a divider with a garden. Along the edge was a steel trash can. She pulled it up out of its metal holder and ran towards the chemist. Fera covered her ears as the bin soared through the air and shattered the front glass window. The noise was as loud as thunder. Delphi kicked out the remaining glass and gingerly stepped inside. Fera removed her hands from her ears and looked at the shards of glass on the ground. When she looked up, Delphi had disappeared between the shelves. She followed her inside.

The Chemist had several shelves in the middle of a large room. Each shelf held multiple boxes and bottles. Delphi picked up the nearest box and read the label. The ingredients were all in gibberish. The letters were jumbled, and some were backwards. Fera walked towards the counter at the rear of the store. It was so quiet and still. It made her feel a little spooked. The countertop was covered in advertisements for medicine, but there weren't specific to any medicine in particular. Photos of families on a picnic, one was looking towards the camera. Also, there were pictures and posters of scenes of people riding horses, or bikes. Everyone was smiling. Delphi appeared by her side, carrying several pill bottles. She plonked them down on the counter. One rolled off the edge and onto the floor.

'They're all empty,' she said.

'All of them?' Fera said, shocked. She turned around and started grabbing items off the nearest shelf. Every box was empty. All the labels were unreadable.

'Why would someone do this? It makes no sense.'

'Keep looking,' Delphi instructed. 'There might be something we need here, anything.'

Fera continued to look around the counter and in the register. Delphi went behind the countertop and up into the chemist area. Lines of shelving held bottles of every size and shape. She knocked them to the ground, hearing them bounce along the linoleum from weightlessness. She swore under her breath. Her frustration started to get the better of her. There was a small fridge tucked in under one of the shelving units. It was empty also, except a small bottle in the door. She picked it up. All that was written on it was *For Spider Bites*. She shook it and could hear several pills rattling around inside.

'I got some gauze and found a half bottle of lotion for scratches,' Fera's voice said, echoing through the pharmacy.

'I found medicine,' Delphi said, staring at the bottle. It was too serendipitous to assume this was put there by chance.

'Great!' Fera yelped in excitement. 'Let's get back to…' As she spoke a roar cut through the open, smashed door. Both girls whipped their head around. It didn't sound human. Heavy footfalls and breath could be heard from outside.

'What was that?' Fera said, almost at a whisper.

Delphi crouched low and headed towards the front of the store. Through the hanging posters and advertisements for fake medicine, she could see the road outside. A huge animal suddenly appeared right in front of her. She gasped and fell backwards, dropping the bottle of medicine on the ground. A lumbering, black bear waddled past the store. Its large legs swayed as it grunted and sniffed the air. Delphi looked back to see Fera heading towards her. She motioned her to get on the ground and stay quiet. The bear paused momentarily, sniffing the air with its shiny, black nose. It opened its mouth and displayed its enormous, pearl-white teeth. Fera spotted the bear as it shambled past the broken glass door panel. She covered her mouth. She wanted to scream. Delphi clutched her around the upper arm and put a finger up to her lips, telling her to be quiet. She could feel her arm shaking.

Something under them shook. It came from under the linoleum floor. Both Delphi and Fera instinctively looked down.

Clank!

Delphi knew that sound all too well now. She looked around, then stood up just in time to see a green ball shoot from on top of the pharmacy building and bounce along the street in front of them.

'Green,' Fera said, watching it roll down the street. 'It means food.'

Delphi looked at Fera quizzically. 'We have to get it.'

'Are you joking?' Fera snapped. 'There's a bear out there.'

'If we don't, we are going to starve after a day or two.'

'We have to get this stuff back to Lyco and worry about the ball later.'

Delphi knew she was right, but deep within her, she still wanted to get it. She craned her neck around the corner, through the smashed door frame. The bear was stopping to sniff a trash can a block further down the road.

'If we run, and make as little noise as possible,' Delphi said looking to Fera, 'I think we can make it across the street.'

Fera looked extremely nervous. 'Then what? What if it sees us? They have better hearing and sense of smell then us.'

Delphi thought for a moment. The only thing that came to mind was Lyco writhing in pain.

'We reach the house across the road and hopefully the door will be unlocked, just like the others. Then we move along, going into each house while keeping an eye on the bear.'

Fera felt her throat tighten. She nodded and took Delphi's hand. Together they crept out of the wreckage of smashed glass and back into the street. The bear had left the trash can and had started to sniff around the general store. Delphi took this chance and started to run. She felt like she was pulling dead weight as Fera struggled to keep up. Fera was holding onto the gauze and medical wipes when her foot hit the curb and she fell forward, tearing herself from Delphi's grip. Her metal leg came loose, flopping to the side. The bear instantly spun its body around, seeing the pair halfway across the street. It started to bolt towards them. Its hairy maw opened to expose gnarled teeth. Its beady black eyes were fixated on them.

'Delphi!' Fera said, seeing the black-haired beast darting towards her. Delphi swept her arms down, juggling the bottle of pills and lifted her up. Fera leant down and strapped her prosthetic leg back into place. Delphi couldn't wait for her to adjust it any longer, she grabbed her shirt and dragged her along the street, pushing her towards the nearest house and ran the other way, flailing her arms in circles. The bear, suddenly confused, altered its path, and headed towards Delphi.

Chapter Three: Blue Moon Light

Fera rushed inside, not hesitating for a moment to see if the door would be locked. Tears streamed down her face as she slammed the door shut behind her. Her breathing was rapid, and she could feel her heartbeat in her neck. She stumbled over to the window and peered outside. Delphi was running for her life, back to the pharmacy.

'Delphi!' Fera screamed. Her voice was trapped inside the house. She looked around panicking and saw a panel right above the fire mantle. It was rectangular shaped with a hole above it. She knew what it was but couldn't connect it with her past. She reached into her pocket and pulled out the steel ball. She marched over to the hole and pushed the ball inside. She could hear it running down a metal ramp, then gears and cogs started to turn. Something clicked loudly followed by machinery moving. All of a sudden, the rectangular outline in the wall popped open like a kitchen drawer. Fera first covered her face, then, when nothing happened, she peered in.

Delphi was pressed up against the glass, knowing she had made a mistake. If the bear got into the pharmacy and wrecked everything, it would blow their chance of possibly finding more medicine. She started to run up the street when she heard a loud horn. The bear, only a few feet behind her moaned in agony. The horn blew again, and the bear started galloping in the other direction. Delphi turned around to see Fera standing in the street, an airhorn in her right hand, held high in the air.

'Delphi!' she screamed. A broad smile lit her face.

Delphi, with barely any energy left, jogged back to Fera

who wrapped her arms around her. Her skin was cold.

'Where did you get that?'

'There was a chute in the house... I used the silver ball.'

Delphi nodded her thanks. She was glad she had used it. Together, they ran back to the house to find Hasse standing out the front, trying to see where they had got to.

'I saw a bear,' she said as the two girls approached. 'I watched it run between the houses and up the embankment towards the forest.'

'It came after us.'

Delphi handed the pills to Hasse. 'How's he doing?'

'He's asleep. I think the pain has subsided a little.'

After a brief rest in the kitchen, Delphi went upstairs to lie down and check for anymore spheres. The house had three bedrooms. All the beds were made and had fresh linen. The mattresses were comfortable and welcoming. The cupboards were empty though and only the bathrooms had running water.

During the night, Lyco had woken in a coughing fit before lying back down and snoring. Delphi and Hasse had gotten up to attend to him. Hasse checked his pulse and attended to some of his wounds he had scratched in his sleep. They stood in the dark house looking out at the empty street cast in blue moonlight.

'I've done this before,' Hasse said, her eyes unfocused.

'It's a game of some sort. I know something needs to be done, like find a door or something.'

Hasse turned to her. She looked tired. 'If that were me out there today, I would have been bear food.'

Delphi gave her a smile, but it was brief. 'The cans won't last long. Tomorrow I'll go with Fera to the general store, and maybe up the street. The town doesn't look that big. We should be able to find something.'

'You mentioned a door,' Hasse said, turning to her. 'I think I remember a door. It's like an old memory, but it's the only one I have.'

'My thoughts are fuzzy. It's like, if I try hard to remember something from my past, it appears clouded in fog. I then feel sick.'

'There is more going on here. We need to be vigilant. If there is a bear around, then there could be other animals.'

Delphi yawned.

'Let's get some sleep.'

Daylight brought with it a cool breeze. The chill permeated through the floorboards and into the house. Fera strolled into the living room with her blanket wrapped around her body. Hasse had divided the cans up into four bowls. Fera ate hers without stopping to take a breath. When Delphi wandered down the stairs, her hair was stuck up at all angles. Fera laughed.

'Be ready in ten minutes if you're coming today,' Delphi said, picking up her bowl.

'Where are we going?'

'To search. For anything. Food, supplies.'

'What about the bear?'

'We'll bring the foghorn and stick to being inside most the time.'

There came a moan from the couch as Lyco sat up. Hasse handed him some tablets and he took them, swallowing them with water.

'Bear?' he mumbled.

'I'll fill you in later, now lie down,' Hasse ordered.

Within the time frame, Fera was ready and waiting by the door. She held the foghorn in her left hand. Delphi nodded to Hasse.

'Take care,' Hasse said, watching them leave with worry on her face.

The sun was up and heating the cold ground when they walked across the wide road to the other side. Fera scanned the surroundings for any sign of the bear. The first house was empty, it had no hole in any of the walls, and no food or water, as did the next two houses. They were identical to the first house, except some were mirrored, or with an extra bedroom or one less. When they got to the general store, Delphi peered through the window as Fera kept watch. She was instantly startled at the sight of a bear on its hind legs. She stepped backwards, her lungs taking in a swift breath of air. Soon, she realised it was a taxidermy bear. Her heart was beating faster. She tried the door, but it was locked.

'I want to go check around the back,' she said to Fera.

'I'm coming with you.'

They walked the length of the red brick wall until they reached a small alleyway. It was long, with no exit doors or ladder to the roof. Delphi was tempted to go all the way down to the end of the road and back up behind the row of houses, but Fera had already started to march down the alleyway. There were old wood crates against the walls. The lids had been pried open and now had bent nails. Fera glanced inside the nearest one, but it was empty. Shredded paper lay on the bottom of them. Whatever had been in there, was long gone. Delphi picked up a plank of wood and held it as they walked. When they reached the end, Delphi sighed in relief. If the bear had cornered them, there would have been no escaping. There was a small field of grass between the houses and the forest. The trees were so close together, it was as if they were trying to stop people from seeing what lay beyond them.

'It's spooky back here,' Fera said, seeing the rear door. It had a glass window with steel bars across it. She stood on her tippy toes and looked inside. 'Seems empty.'

Delphi tried the door, and it was unlocked. She pushed it and it creaked open, as if it had been shut tight for fifty years and had started to rust. Inside was a small room with a desk covered in dust, a mop with a frayed cloth end and gumboots covered in mud. Fera shut the door as they both entered and went over to the boots.

'Does that mud look fresh to you?'

Delphi knelt down and ran her finger across the side of the boot. It dropped off in a wet, sludge.

'It's very fresh… but there's been no rain.'

'I don't like that,' Fera said, her eyes full of fear.

'Let's keep going.'

There was a small hallway with one door on the right. At the very end of the corridor were twin swinging doors. Delphi could see the shop floor through the glass view panel. She walked in front till they reached midway where the door was. Written on a plaque was Office. She tried the handle and it turned. Peaking inside, she could see another desk, covered in dust and old spiderwebs. The floor was carpet. It was old and had been wet at some point in its life. She could smell its rancid odour. She slid inside and pulled all the drawers out. There were blank pieces of paper, an old typewriter with no ink and an old coffee mug with dried coffee in the bottom of it. She re-shut the door and moved along to the showroom. Before pushing the swinging doors open, both girls pushed up on their tippytoes and scanned the room for any sign of movement. Fera looked at Delphi.

'Looks clear?'

'We'll go slow and quiet until we can be sure,' just as Fera went to push the door open, Delphi told her about the taxidermy bear. Fera felt her gut sink and let Delphi go first.

The door swung open and both girls slid into the store. It smelled of freshly oiled wood and stale air. Delphi did a quick look around and couldn't see anyone. She stood up and walked to the centre of the room.

'Delphi,' Fera said, looking up at the giant bear. 'I really don't like this place.'

'Look for anything worth taking and we'll get out of here.'

Delphi looked at the products hanging on hooks, but they were all empty. They were labelled fishing hooks and line and bait, but the boxes and plastic containers were all fake and empty. Fera saw a large freezer to the right of the store. Across the top it read Fish Bait. Delphi walked behind the counter and checked under the register and in all the drawers. She found more blank pieces of paper, a pen that didn't work and a hairbrush, which she slid into her pocket. A scream split the stillness of the store. It was from Fera. Delphi got up so fast she nearly hit her head on an open cupboard drawer. She ran out, towards Fera's voice. She could see her suddenly drop the freezer door down and step away. Her face was pale white, and she was shaking. Delphi grabbed her.

'What is it, Fera?'

'There's someone in there!'

Delphi pushed Fera behind her and stepped forward. Fera clutched her elbow and tried to pull her back.

'Don't do it, Delphi!'

Delphi gingerly opened the freezer door. There was a body wrapped in plastic, frozen to death, curled up at the bottom of the freezer. Delphi shut it and turned to Fera.

'Let's go, quick,' She ran towards the rear of the door.

Once outside, Delphi found it hard to get a lungful of air. Panic had stricken her incapable. She bent forwards, her hands on her knees, while she sucked in oxygen.

'Who was that?' Fera asked, trying not to gag.

'I don't know. Looks like he might be the owner of the mud boots though.'

'Why do you say that?'

Delphi stood up. 'I saw mud around the bottom of his pants.'

'This place is getting to me, Delphi.'

'I know, Fera. We have to keep moving, no matter what we see.'

Delphi gathered herself and kept moving up the rear of the store. There was a ladder towards the southern end. She stopped and looked up towards the roof.

'We might be able to get a better understanding of what's around here,' she noted.

'And maybe give someone a chance to see us,' Fera said.

Delphi wasn't sure if that was good or bad. She began to climb up the ladder and stepped onto the roof. It was flat, grey concrete with a rusted air conditioning system in the right corner. From atop the store, they could see the town in its entirety. It went on for far longer than they both first thought. At the end of the main thoroughfare, the street split into two, right and left. There was a big building, several stories high at the very end of the town, as well as what looked to be a lighthouse or tower. To the right, were several more houses and smaller buildings. Streetlights lined the footpaths.

'Look,' Fera said, pointing far in the distance. 'A car.'

Delphi could see the small red vehicle parked in a parking lot beside a massive square building.

'Maybe we can start it, and get out of here?'

'Maybe it's a trap too,' Delphi said.

'We won't be able to tell until we take a look,' Fera pleaded.

Delphi looked at her and could see how rattled she was. There was a good chance she just wanted to get away from the general store.

'Okay, let's go take a look.'

They climbed back down and cut through a side road back to the main road. Delphi looked out for the bear. When she couldn't see any signs of it, she waved Fera to join her. The road was starting to warm their bare feet. Fera stopped and adjusted her prosthetic metal leg, taking it off and repositioning it. She did it like she had done it a million times before. She didn't say anything the whole time and Delphi didn't bring attention to it. Fera stood up and walked a few feet, nodding that her readjusting of the leg was acceptable. The clouds above moved with slow intention, moving east. From behind them they could suddenly hear the whooping of something in the sky. They both turned and covered their eyes from the glaring sun.

'What is that?'

'It doesn't sound like a bird,' Delphi replied, scanning the sky.

A dot along the skyline, many kilometres away, had a vague outline of something that triggered their memory.

'Is it a plane?'

'It looks like a helicopter.'

They watched it circle around, coming closer, then make a sharp turn and disappearing into the sun.

'Maybe there's more of us out there?'

'I'm not sure if it would be a good thing to find them or stay hidden.'

Fera shrugged, turning back to the road. 'Maybe they'll find us first.'

With the sun at their backs, they continued marching up the main street.

Chapter Four: Bumper

They had reached the end of the road. The sun was high in the sky and the clouds lingered as if watching them from afar. Delphi looked left, towards the car. There was no movement, only the whistle from a slight breeze in between the houses. She looked right, towards the larger building. It was the only building with multi-levels. Fera had the foghorn still in her hand. Her knuckles were turning white from her grip.

'Why are we stopping?' Fera said.

'I thought I heard something,' Delphi answered.

Fera stood dead still as she tried to listen for something, anything. There was a strange humming and then the noise of something big moving, like heavy tires. It was coming from under them.

'Let's keep going.'

Every house they passed felt like someone was watching them through the window. Every few steps Delphi would stop and look behind her, expecting to see someone standing there, but there never was. The row of houses suddenly ended with a large car park. It had room for hundreds of cars, but only one was in it. Large lamp posts stood every ten spaces, their covers and bulbs missing. Delphi and Fera stopped a few meters short of the vehicle. Its windows were foggy, so they couldn't see in. Delphi knew it was an older model car. She didn't know how she knew it, but she did.

'Should we open the door?' Fera asked, looking to Delphi for confirmation.

She thought there may be something inside worth taking. Delphi took the last few steps towards the car and stared into it, seeing if she could get a better view of the interior. She couldn't see anything. It was too blurry through the greasy windows.

'It's smudged on the inside,' she said. 'As if someone didn't want us to see in.'

'Stand back,' Fera said. 'I'll open it'.

Delphi looked at her and was surprised by her sudden outburst of confidence. Giving into Fera's instructions, Delphi did as she was asked and stood behind her. Gingerly, she reached out and gripped the door handle and pulled it. It creaked open on rusted hinges. The driver's seat was empty. It was an antique car with torn leather seats. The dashboard had started to peel, and flecks of plastic and leather were on the seat and footrests. There were scratch marks across the windscreen as if someone had tried to smash it with something to get out.

'I'll check inside the glovebox,' Fera said, suddenly feeling relieved.

She glanced in the back seat and saw that it was covered in multiple snakes. She screamed and launched herself backwards. The snakes poured over the seat and between the gear shifter, slithering out the open door and onto the warm ground. Delphi grabbed Fera and pulled her back. She could feel her whole body shaking.

'I hate snakes!' she screamed, clutching onto Delphi with all her strength.

They watched the snakes lift their heads and lash their tongues out, sniffing the air.

'That isn't just snakes looking for food in there, someone put them all in there. It looks like whenever someone puts pressure on the seat, they are released from the trunk.'

The largest of the snakes was several meters long with a bright yellow underbelly. Its head was as big as Fera's fist. It barely gave them a glance as it slithered off in the direction of the forest.

'I'll check the glovebox,' Delphi said. 'Stay here.'

'Wait!' Fera shouted. 'Don't. There could be something else in there.'

Delphi walked around to the other side of the car, careful to avoid stepping on any stray snakes still pondering where to go. She opened the door and put her hand on the glovebox. She glanced up at Fera, who looked utterly terrified. Delphi swung it open fast and pulled her hand away just in time as a cobra lashed out, its fangs poised. Delphi screamed and rushed back. The cobra fell to the floor of the vehicle and slunk its way over the edge of the car and under it. Delphi leant over and could see a green sphere nestled in the glovebox. She reached in and snatched it as quickly as she could. She held it up for Fera to see. She was still traumatized and could barely gather a smile. Delphi slipped it into her pocket, and they began to venture up the street. Fera's heart was still pounding out of her chest, but after a few minutes of walking, she slowly started to gather herself.

'What's that noise?' Fera said, after a few minutes walking.

Delphi listened and could barely hear it. 'Sounds like a humming. Like something is revving. It sounds like the noise we heard earlier… but closer.'

From ahead of them, came a cacophonous roar as another car sped around the corner and headed straight for them.

'It's coming this way!' Delphi said.

Fera turned and bolted, as did Delphi. The car was gaining speed rapidly. As they zigzagged across the street, the car followed their every move. Soon it was upon them, rocketing at an enormous speed.

'Fera, watch out!' Delphi roared, pushing her out of the way as the car narrowly missed her.

Its bumper clipped Delphi's hip and sent her rolling across the ground. The car spun straight into a lamp pole. The windows smashed out and the hood flew open. The engine suddenly burst into flames. Fera ran over to her and knelt down.

'Are you okay?' she said, her voice in a panic.

'Yeah, I think so,' Delphi replied, wincing. She tried to move, but her hip hurt.

They looked towards the flaming wreckage. Delphi slowly got to her feet with help from Fera. She hobbled towards the flaming wreckage, covering her face from the heat, and tried to see who or what was driving it. The closer she got, the more the flames licked the air and hot oil popped and spat. The driver's seat was empty.

'I think we should go back,' Fera announced, feeling uneasy.

'I agree,' Delphi replied. 'I don't think I can take much more today.'

Together they slowly inched their way home. The bear was nowhere to be seen, but they still kept to the shadows, occasionally ducking into a house if they heard a noise. Once they got in view of the house, they saw Lyco and Hasse out the front waving them in. They were holding up something.

'I can't see it,' Fera said, looking at them with narrowed eyes.

'They probably found more food,' Delphi wondered. She didn't much care at this point. Her hip was throbbing, and she felt like her skin was fried from the explosion.

'We got one!' Hasse said, ecstatically.

'You got a ball?' Delphi said, amazed.

Once they saw Delphi was hobbling, Lyco ran to the stairs to help her, but Hasse pulled him back, knowing he was still in pain. They got Delphi to the couch where Lyco had laid.

'This must be the medical lounge,' Lyco said.

'What happened?'

'A car hit me.'

'A car? Was someone in it?'

Fera plonked herself down on a spare chair and reached for the half empty bottle of water.

'There are wild animals out there… and,' she paused.

'And?' Hasse waited, her hands on her hips.

'Someone is dead in the general store,' Delphi finished her sentence.

Lyco looked at Hasse upset. 'What do you mean? Did you kill them?'

'No,' Fera shouted. 'They were already dead. They're in the freezer.'

They told them about the bear and snakes and then Delphi reached into her pocket and pulled out a green ball.

'We did manage to get this though,' she held it up so the sunlight pouring in through the window caught it and made it gleam. 'Now tell us,' she said, sitting up. 'How did you get yours?'

Hasse held the silver ball in her hand. 'Well,' she started, 'Lyco had gotten up and started to walk around, so I went upstairs to the bathroom to get more water when I heard it… *clunk!*' she made the all too familiar noise.

'It came out of the bathroom somewhere?'

'No, it was in the wall, so I followed it. Then I heard Lyco screaming from downstairs, I thought he had hurt himself again, but he could hear it. So, I ran down to join him and it shot out of the fireplace.'

Delphi and Fera both turned their heads to look at the fire mantle.

'The next-door house has the chute, maybe it's every second house?'

'That's gonna make it hard for us to get any more spheres.'

'They're trying to split us up,' Lyco added, sitting down.

Hasse stood in the middle of the room, as if she was the leader.

'I think we need to get out of this house and move further up the street. We saw some bigger buildings,' Delphi said, placing her head on a pillow.

'I say we lock down tonight, and all stay here. Delphi is hurt and Lyco is still in pain,' Hasse added. 'If you want, we can take turns keeping watch. We don't know if more animals will come, or if more balls will be released.'

'Good idea,' Lyco said.

'Tomorrow, we'll go together. No more splitting up.'

Before Fera had even gotten to the hallway to find a room, she could hear Delphi fast asleep.

Chapter Five: Gentle Hum

Lyco rolled over. Hasse was beside him in bed. She had been afraid to sleep on her own so she had asked him through the night if she could lay beside him. He slowly got to his feet and went to the bathroom. With the small amount of light coming in through the window, from the half moon, he could see his reflection in the mirror. He leant closer, inspecting his face. The bite marks were going down and he was feeling close to normal, except all his joints still throbbed. He splashed water on his face and went downstairs. Fera was standing by the window. She had the curtain wrapped around her body, for warmth and to hide from anyone that might be looking in. Lyco had made certain to make a small amount of noise, so he didn't frighten her. She turned and looked at him standing in the blue-black darkness.

'Lyco?'

'Yes, it's me.'

'What are you doing up? It's Delphi's turn to keep watch.'

He walked closer to her, so he wouldn't wake Delphi, who was still asleep on the couch.

'I couldn't sleep. Probably because I slept earlier.'

There was a warmth to him that Fera couldn't quite find the reason for. She guessed it was his kind nature. He stood beside her and looked out onto the empty road.

'Anything?'

'No, not a thing. Not even a bird or a bat.'

'Strange. Now you say it, I didn't see a bird the whole time we were coming down the hill.'

'What do you think happened to them?'

'I don't know,' Lyco shrugged. 'Maybe they fear to come near this place? Maybe they're all gone.'

Fera looked back out the window, 'I hope not.'

They stood in silence for a while.

'You should get some sleep,' he finally said.

'What about Delphi?'

'I'm awake,' said a slightly groggy voice from the lounge. Delphi sat up and moved her hair from her face. 'Must be my watch by now?'

'I can do it,' Lyco offered.

'No, it's okay,' she said, standing up and stretching. 'You need the rest. The tablets could make you drowsy. Go back to bed.'

Lyco wanted to debate, but he still wanted to rest his joints. 'Okay,' he finally said and turned to head back to the stairs.

Fera walked over to the couch and went to lay down.

'Find a room, Fera,' Delphi said, putting her hair up in a ponytail. 'The couch is not great for your back. My hip is killing me.'

Fera lay on the couch for a minute and tossed and turned and decided she was right.

'If you need me, I'll be in the last room. Yell out if you see something.'

'I will.'

Delphi watched Fera stroll off into the darkness. She pulled the right side of her pant leg up and saw a bruise forming. She walked a few steps to test her hip from sleeping on the couch. She turned and walked back to the window. It hurt, but it wasn't too painful. She looked out the window to the houses across the street and waited for something to move, anything.

The night was dark and still. Towards the top of the street, she could just see the general store. There was something about the store that stuck in her mind like a thorn. It was like they had interrupted something happening, or they were meant to find something. Delphi struggled with her impulse before caving into temptation. She marched to the door and unlocked it, slowly creeping outside into the cold night. Her skin broke into gooseflesh. It felt like she was the only one left in the world. She went down into the front yard and promised herself she would be quick. No longer than twenty minutes. She ran across the street as fast as she could and up to the next block. She slid down the alley way and around the back. The rear of the store was pitch black. She had to fumble her way down the hallway to the shop floor. She could hear the gentle hum of the freezer where the body was. She crept through the aisles, careful not to make a noise. When she reached the freezer, she gently opened it. Cold air wafted up from the container. She could see the curled-up body inside, in the foetal position. Slowly, she reached in. Her fingers long and inching towards the dead body. Ever so gently, she patted the person down, feeling for anything in its pockets. The plastic was freezing cold and wet. Then, as she glided past its left hip pocket, she could feel something inside. It was round. She pulled the plastic to the side, revealing its clothes. It looked male. Then, from behind her, she could hear voices. There were two and they were rushed and aggressive. She looked around quickly for somewhere to hide, but she could now hear them marching down the hallway. At any second, they would burst through the swinging doors and catch her. She climbed into the freezer and shut the lid.

'…how were we to know they would get this far?' a voice said.

'The last group didn't even come in here.'

'What do you think they'll do to us?'

Then there was silence. Delphi could feel the dead man's hand against her spine.

'I don't want to end up in here.'

'Even if you had been, you wouldn't remember.'

'I'd remember. I remember everything.'

'Not this.'

'Let's get it so we can get out of here.'

Footsteps moved from the middle of the room, then over

to the freezer. Delphi held her breath as she saw the container lid open. A third voice suddenly appeared in the room.

'Scrap it!' a female voice shouted. 'We need help with the boat... Come back to this later, the body ain't going anywhere.'

The lid slammed shut, making Delphi jump in fright. The rumble of multiple legs rushed out of the room. She could her the doors swinging, and the back door shut. She breathed a sigh of relief. She quickly leaped out of the freezer. Her skin felt like it was crawling. She turned back and reached into the man's pocket, snatching at the object. She held it up, another silver ball. She ran to the door and peered through. There was no sign of anyone. She moved quickly through the darkness to the rear door and scanned around the surrounding area. Far up the mountain she could see torchlight. They were heading away from her. She moved along the wall and back down between the house and the store.

In the morning they all gathered in the lounge. Their bellies were rumbling, and they all looked sleep deprived. Much to their chagrin, Delphi explained what she had done and showed them the silver ball.

'You shouldn't go out by yourself,' Hasse said. She sounded mad.

'If something happened to you, we wouldn't know till morning.'

Delphi knew they were right. 'Okay, I promise not to do it again,' she said, placing the silver ball down on the coffee table. Fera got her ball out and placed it beside it.

'Shall we go next door and see what the chute gives us?' Lyco said, clearly feeling much better since taking the tablets.

Hasse straightened the cushions before they left and placed the empty cans in the bin. They paused at the door, all looking through the windows to make sure the bear, or anything else, wasn't around. Then they made their way to the next house. It was set up exactly the same as the house they had just left, however, the only difference was the chute above the fireplace. They gathered around and let Fera step forward with her silver ball. She plopped it into the entrance hole and stood back. Gears and cogs wound and twisted beneath them. Metal chains rattled and pulled something heavy. Then there was a loud plonk as something fell into the chute, like a giant vending machine dropping an enormous candy bar. The draw popped open with vicious intent. Fera stepped towards it and glanced inside. She didn't move. Delphi looked over to Lyco and Hasse. They too were waiting.

'Fera?' Delphi said. 'What's in it?'

Fera glanced down so they could see the shock in her face. She reached in and pulled out a long-handled shovel. There was a tag on the end that read *Bury Your Dead.* She pulled it out and held it out for someone to take. Lyco stepped forward and took it from her.

'They want us to bury that person you found in the freezer?'

'Or when one of us dies?'

Fera slammed the chute closed. She stood back to let Delphi place her ball in. The room went dead quiet. Delphi positioned her ball in the opening. She heard it slide down its metal gullet and clank against rails. The ball could be heard swivelling from left to right, before dropping down out of earshot. Rolling chains came from above. Everyone looked up. The chute suddenly popped opened, and everyone jumped in fright. Delphi reached inside. She turned around, holding a roughly drawn map.

Hasse bent over to study it. It was drawn with pencil with crudely sketched arrows leading through the town. It ended with an 'X'.

'A way out?'

'Possibly,' Lyco said. 'Or a trap?'

'How can we know unless we go there?' Fera said.

'I say we go, but we go carefully, maybe watch the area from afar first?'

The others nodded their agreement.

Fera reached into her pocket and pulled out the green ball. She held it up for the others to see.

'Do we save it? Or use it now.'

'I'm pretty hungry,' Lyco said.

'Let me look around first, there may be something here?' Hasse began her search of the house. She looked in all the cupboards, and in every room. There was nothing else. They drank the one water bottle they had and refilled it.

'You do it,' Fera said, handing the ball to Lyco.

He took it and walked it over to the chute, as if it were a delicate egg. He let it rest of the hole lip and then dropped it in. They didn't bother looking up this time, instead they waited for the familiar clank of the chute being closed from the inside. When it came, Lyco yanked the chute open. They all peered in. Inside was a small bag of salted peanuts. He placed his hand in gingerly and pulled it out for the others to see.

'They really don't like feeding us, do they?'

They split the nuts up so everyone got five each and they ate them and felt even for hungrier than before.

Out on the road, gloomy, heavy clouds ambled across the sky. Rain was on its way.

'Stop outside the general store, before we get too far,' Delphi said, now holding the shovel.

'You're not serious about…'

'If that's what they want us to do, I say we do it,' Delphi said, cutting her off.

'I'll come with you,' Lyco said, looking to Hasse.

'I don't think I could bear witness to a dead body.'

'You stay out here, with Fera. Keep watch and we'll do it,' Lyco said, putting his hand on Hasse's shoulder.

'Don't be too long.'

Lyco nodded and turned to follow Delphi. They walked down the thin alleyway that Delphi had already walked several times before.

'Did you want to scout around before we take the body out?' Lyco said.

'We looked around, me and Fera, and we couldn't find anything. But, if you don't think Hasse will panic, we can take a quick look.'

Lyco wasn't keen on burying a body either, but his stomach was starting to rumble. They entered the general store and could smell a pungent odour. Lyco gagged slightly in his throat. Delphi pulled her shirt up over her nose and headed for the freezer, without waiting for Lyco. The store floor seemed untouched still. Lyco scouted around shelves and inside drawers. He found a safe in the rear room behind a painting that Delphi had previously neglected to look behind. The safe was locked.

'Delphi!' he yelled for her, but there was no answer. Suddenly he became very fearful.

He turned and rushed from the room and could see Delphi looking into the freezer. She looked like a statue, unmoving.

'I'll come help you pull him out.'

'Don't bother,' she said. 'There's no one in here.'

Lyco glanced over her shoulder. The freezer was empty.

'Are you sure this was where the body was?'

'Yes, it's the only freezer in here.'

'The people you overheard. You said something about them taking it?'

'I'm not sure,' she said, closing the lid. Her face was still crestfallen. 'It means the shovel is for burying one of us.'

Lyco put his hands on her shoulder. 'Not necessarily. Whoever these people are, they are playing with our heads. Remember that.'

Chapter Six: Massacre

Hasse and Fera waited outside the general store. They were scanning the roads up and down for any sign of animals.

'If that bear comes back, I can't outrun it' Hasse said, looking nervous.

'I don't think any of us can, including Delphi.'

'Let's hope they are quick.'

'I really don't like this place,' Hasse added, slightly under her breath.

'It's not a real town, as far as my memory goes. Towns should have real people, walking around, not quiet streets.'

Delphi and Lyco emerged from the alleyway. Fera and Hasse looked over to them with sadness on their faces.

'It wasn't there,' Delphi said, relieving them of their tension.

'Where did he go?'

'They probably took him away last night?'

Delphi dug the map out from her pocket. 'We need to get going. We're all hungry and sticking around this area too long.'

'Agreed' Fera added.

The map took them up the street and left, away from the first car. There was no sign of snakes except for a shredded snakeskin they found wrapped around one of the street poles. The second car, that had burst into flames, was gone. The only memento of it being there were scorch marks on the concrete and across the wall. They walked past with unease.

They were all dead quiet as they took the next right and could see the town open up before them. There was a large, paved area ahead with a water feature. Water was bubbling out of a statue that was holding a large seashell. On either side of the town centre were older buildings, made of mostly wood. They gathered at the entrance and glanced around, checking for movement or anything suspicious. The sun was hot and hung above them like a boiled egg.

'I want to go to the waterfall, see if we can drink the water.'

'I wouldn't, Fera,' Lyco said. 'Who knows what is in it.'

Fera didn't particularly like being told what to do. She huffed her cheeks out and stepped on the paved, circular area. Delphi looked at the map.

'It takes us through here and to the other end.'

Lyco looked at the map, then up to the horizon. He could see a tower. He looked back to the map.

'Looks like a lighthouse?'

Fera had sat down to readjust her prosthetic leg. It was sweaty and had started to irritate her.

'Let's look around here for food.'

'I'll go with Delphi,' Fera said, strapping the metal and plastic leg back on.

Lyco nodded and together with Hasse, they went to the nearest, multi-storey shopfront. The sign above the door was blank. There had been something there though. Lyco could see old screw marks and different colouration in the paint. He pushed the front door open and stepped inside. Hasse held onto the rear of his shirt. She feared being ambushed by animals.

'Looks like an old farm-house?' Lyco stated. 'A place that used to sell food for livestock.'

Hasse glanced around Lyco's large frame. There were several bags of horse feed leaning against the wall. Some were marked with prices and feed type. To the right was a horse made of fibreglass with a leather saddle on it. Hasse's inherent interest got the better of her and she found herself steadily walking over to it. She ran her hand along the leather. A vague familiarity washed over her.

'I think… as a kid I had a horse?' she said, quietly. Lyco

was searching around the checkout area and hadn't heard her. 'It was a big one… I sort of remember. I was scared to ride it.'

Pain sparked in her head, and she winced and stepped away. When she looked up, she could see a wooden staircase at the rear of the shop, heading up to the next level. Something told her to go up. She looked over to Lyco who was rifling through paperwork. He seemed preoccupied. She looked back at the stairs and saw a foot disappear from view and heard soft running.

'Hello?' she said. 'Is someone here?' There was no answer. *Maybe it was one of the girls, coming through a rear entrance? Maybe they're being chased,* she thought.

'Lyco, I'm going upstairs for a minute.' Her voice was meek and powerless.

She hurried through the store and slowed when she approached the stairs. She looked up to see someone move across the doorframe. They had long hair and were about Fera's height.

'Fera? Everything okay?' She hesitated for a moment, checking to see if Lyco was following her, but she couldn't see him. 'Fera? Delphi?' there was nerves in her voice. She went up the stairs, one by one, steadily, and slowly. The doorway ahead of her, once past the doorframe, only showed a blank wall. It appeared to be a hallway.

'Fera?'

Lyco tried to read the paper he found by an old laptop. It was gibberish. A mixture of words and numbers. Some of the letters were backwards. He opened the laptop and tried to start it, but it was dead. He picked it up and looked under it. There was a serial number, but it didn't make any sense, so he placed it back on the desk. He slid his hand under the desk behind the counter and found a secret draw. He pulled it out and laying in a plastic packet was some dried fruit. He picked it up and held it up to the light. It was shrivelled and curled. He opened it and sniffed the contents. It smelt delicious. He slid it in his pocket. A scream cut through the store. His head whipped around were Hasse had been.

'Hasse?' he called out, quickly running around the countertop. 'Hasse?'

She was nowhere to be seen. He had heard her speaking, but he wasn't listening properly. He thought she was marvelling at the saddle, something about owning a horse.

'Hasse!' he called again and heard the pounding of footsteps upstairs. He ran to the staircase and took it two at a time. As he reached the top level, a door slammed in his face and he heard it being locked.

'Let me in!' he demanded, pounding on the door with his fists. From under the door slid a note. He yanked it from someone's grasp and read it. It was an address. He looked at the door and tried to kick it, then smashed it with his fists. But it was solid wood.

Fera stood in front of the waterfall and cupped her hands in the flowing water. She drunk it as Delphi watched her. She swished it around her mouth and swallowed it. She waited for a few seconds, to see if her stomach rejected it, but nothing happened.

'How was it?' Delphi asked, a small grin appearing on her face.

'Tastes fine to me. Tastes like water.'

'We'll see in an hour or two.'

'Where do you want to go first?'

Delphi looked up the street. There was a multi-level department store. A sign in big red letters above it read, *Norway's.*

'How about there?'

Fera looked at the building, then back at the place Hasse and Lyco had gone.

'What if they come out and we're not here.'

'We won't be long. We'll look at the first two levels. Besides, they'll probably be a while. That building is pretty large.'

They walked side by side, listening for danger until they were standing in front of the store. The front door was a revolving door. The glass was dirty and smudged with grease. Delphi stepped into the turnstile and pushed against the metal frame. It slowly began to turn. She waited on the other side for Fera. In front of them was an escalator going up to the next level. To the left was an open showroom full of mannequins. None of them were dressed. Their white, plastic bodies were held in a model poses, with blank eyes and expressionless faces.

'This is too creepy,' Fera said.

To the right appeared to be perfume and make-up.

'The nights are getting colder. We should look for warmer clothing also.'

'Let's start over there,' Fera said, pointing towards the mannequins. Approaching them, Fera felt like they were going to leap on top of her. Their alien eyes and long fingers gave them a horrific appearance. They moved through the clothing section. All the racks were empty. Clothes hangers were lopsided and scattered on the floor. Delphi could see torn clothes tossed into the corners, as if someone had been there before them and ruined whatever had been left behind. There was a full-length mirror attached to a pillar in the middle of the showroom. Fera stood in front of it.

'I need to eat,' she said, seeing how her pants were sagging.

Delphi looked deeper into the store and saw the changing rooms. She headed towards them. Fera was going to follow but found herself magnetised towards the perfume and make-up.

Delphi checked each change room, one after the other. In the last room, behind the door hung a fur coat. Its price tag was still on, but the numbers were gibberish. She slid it on and looked at herself in the mirror. It wasn't something she thought she would normally wear, but if it got colder, it would come in handy.

Fera strolled down the long isle of perfume bottles. They were all gorgeous looking bottles. All different shapes and sizes with a small hand pump. Fera picked one up and smelt the spray tip. It didn't smell like anything. She sniffed it again, then turned it towards her neck and pumped the spray. A green mist sprayed from the spout in a cloud. Her vison went instantly fuzzy, and she stepped back, dropping the glass bottle on the ground. It shattered everywhere, sending shards of glass and green ooze over the polished tile floor. Fera tangled her feet and tried to steady herself. She tried to scream, but her mouth only gurgled. She fell to the floor in an unconscious slump.

Delphi had found a small room at the rear of the store when she heard the smashing of glass. She looked up.

'Fera?' she yelled. When there was no response, she ran out from the room. 'Fera!'

Still no answer. She ran back through the mannequins. Some of them looked like they had moved position. She called her name again, but there was still no response. When she got to the escalators, she went into the perfume section. On the ground was a smashed perfume bottle. Delphi leant down in her fur coat and examined it. She looked around but could not see Fera anywhere.

'Fera!'

When she walked along the other side, she could see gleams of green footprints leading back to the escalator.

'She must have thought I was upstairs,' Delphi said and proceeded up at the stalled escalator. The metal teeth were sharp and threatened to cut her shins if she tripped.

Once at the top she could see hundreds of mannequins. Although she couldn't remember stores like this, is seemed far too many.

'Fera!' she tried again. At the rear of the 2nd level, through the mannequins, she could hear a muffled scream.

Delphi started to run, her fur coat wavering behind her. She pushed over mannequins as she bolted through them. Shoving them to the side, they fell and clattered against one another. The domino effect started a small wave of life size dolls toppling over, arms started to come off and legs popped from the hips. Suddenly she was in a strange clearing with nothing around her but a wall of glass. Inside, a black mist swirled and touched the glass, eager to escape.

'Fera! Delphi! Hasse!' came a familiar voice from behind her. It was coming from the direction of the escalator she had just climbed.

Lyco came rocketing up the staircase. He paused for a moment, viewing the carnage of the tumbled over mannequins. It looked like a massacre. In his hands he held the piece of paper with the address to the department store. He dropped it onto the ground.

'Delphi!' he cried out as he ran to her, dodging arms and legs strewn across the ground. 'Hasse is missing, you gotta come help…' his words seized as he came into view of the glass wall. 'What is this? Where's Fera?'

The black smoke was suddenly sucked out of the glass cage, exposing the rectangular room dividing it into two by a glass wall. Hasse was on the right, lying on the ground and Fera on the left, unconscious.

Chapter Seven: To Nowhere

Delphi mashed on the glass with her closed fist. The glass wobbled but didn't crack. She ran to the mannequins and snatched a displaced arm and ran back to the glass cage. She hammered the arm across the wall with full force, but it didn't even make a mark. Lyco went and picked up a mannequin that happened to stay in one piece and threw it at the glass, to no effect. It simply bounced off and rattled along the ground, landing by his feet.

'What is going on? Hasse!'

Hasse slowly started to regain consciousness.

'Lyco? Delphi? Where am I?'

'Stay still,' Delphi said desperately. 'We'll try get you out!'

'Delphi, look,' Lyco said, suddenly moving away from the glass wall. He knelt down and pointed, looking up at Delphi. 'Holes.' There was one in front of Hasse and one in front of Fera.

'We don't have any balls left,' Delphi said through gritted teeth.

Fera sat up and looked around. Through the middle glass wall, she could see Hasse looking very worried and confused. She stood up to see Delphi and Lyco looking at her through the front glass pane.

'Fera,' Lyco said, moving over to her glass cage. 'Don't panic. We'll get you out.'

Fera nodded, too afraid to speak. Something fell from her pocket as she moved around the small encasement. She bent down and picked it up. It was a piece of paper. Delphi saw her reading it and walked to her with restrained calm. Fera read the note and a tear dropped from her eye. She walked to the wall and planted it flat across the pane so they could read it: *Choose One.*

'How can we choose one?' Lyco said, standing in front of Hasse. 'We don't have any spheres,' his heart was beginning to sink.

Suddenly, both the glass rooms started refilling with black smoke. Fera bashed her hands on the glass in front of Delphi.

'Help me!' she screamed. 'Get me out of here!'

Lyco ran to the escalator and back down to the first floor. He searched for something heavier, or sharper to break the glass.

Hasse placed one palm on the glass. Her fingers were spread wide. She looked dejected, but stoic.

'It's okay, Delphi. Let me go, save Fera.'

'No, Hasse,' Delphi said, tears emerging from her eyes as she watched the smog encompass the rooms.

The two women were barely visible now.

'Delphi…help,' Fera's voice was staggered as she started to choke on the smoke.

Delphi picked up a mannequin leg and belted the glass over and over, her frustration getting the better of her. Downstairs, Lyco kicked open a hallway door and saw a fire extinguisher attached to the wall by a metal bracket. He tore it from its holder and ran back upstairs. Delphi was on her knees in front of Fera's glass cage. Her head was down, and her hand was on the glass.

'I choose,' she said, her voice depressed.

Lyco blinked away tears as he rushed towards Hasse's smoke-filled room and threw the extinguisher through the front panel. The wall, weakened by the numerous hits, suddenly smashed into a thousand pieces. The noise inside the store sounded like a gunshot. Lyco marched in, fearless of getting glass in his feet. He waved his arms around wildly, trying to clear the smoke.

'Hasse!' there was panic in his voice.

The smog was suddenly sucked through vents in the ceiling to reveal an empty room. In the room beside him, Fera was slumped against a wall, her knees brought up to her chest. Her eyes were closed.

'Fera!' Delphi yelped, mashing her fists on the glass.

Lyco saw a thin veil of a door in the dividing wall. He pushed it, ready to fetch his extinguisher, but the door popped open, seemingly on its own. He rushed in with Delphi close behind him. He picked up Fera, cradling her in his arms.

'Let's get out of here, we don't want to get trapped as well.'

They made their way back down the escalator and out the front spinning door. The sun was high above them. Lyco found a bench beside one of the corner stores. It was in the shade, so he lay Fera on it and knelt down beside her.

'Fera?'

She opened her eyes and started coughing. Delphi pulled the water bottle from her pocket and gave it to Lyco who helped her drink from it.

'What happened?' she said, sitting up, still choking the black smoke out of her throat.

'I turned around and you were gone…' Delphi said. 'Last I saw you were right behind me.'

Fera wiped her hair away from her face. 'I was in the perfume section…' she suddenly stopped and looked around at Lyco and Delphi. 'Where's Hasse?'

Lyco looked at Delphi and stood up. His face said it all.

'We had to choose,' Delphi said, trying to stop tears from brewing in her eyes.

'Choose? What do you mean? Between me and Hasse?'

Delphi nodded her response.

'And you chose me? Why?'

Delphi took a defensive step back. She couldn't answer her question.

'Come on,' Lyco finally said. 'What's done is done. What's important is that we get out of here. We can figure this all out later. We didn't see her body, so they just took her away.'

'*They*,' Fera said, getting to her feet. She tested her prosthetic leg by leaning gently on it.

They gathered themselves and started the journey through the town centre and out the other side. None of them spoke for some time. They were all thinking of Hasse. The sun moved across the sky as they passed several more blocks of houses, identical to the last block where they had just walked past. It was starting to feel as if they were walking in circles. Shortly after this thought entered Delphi's mind, they reached the very edge of the houses. Towards the very edge of the incline, was a hill with a lighthouse.

'That's where the map leads,' Lyco said, his voice still crestfallen.

'Look,' Fera said, running a few steps towards what she thought was another water feature.

Delphi followed her and could see it was a large hole in the ground. It was rimmed with a metal brace, with large, pivoted bolts. Haphazard welding marks were strewn across it, attaching it to the central gutter. It was nearly five feet in diameter. Delphi knelt down and looked inside its steely oesophagus. It seemed to go on for ever until a bend in the tube made it impossible to see.

'What do you think?' Lyco said. 'Do we jump down it?'

'Is it a way out?'

'It's not on the map.'

'What if it leads to nowhere?'

Delphi knew they were out of coloured balls, so she looked around for anything to throw down it. She found a few rocks, that were as close to being round as she could get.

'If it leads to danger, or to a room, hopefully we hear it,' Delphi said, pinching a rock between her thumb and forefinger. She dropped it and they all watched it spin in the air and hit the metal gullet. It slid for a few meters before starting to roll. Everyone was dead quiet while they listened to it spin and crack against the sides. It slid and tumbled out of view. The sound was getting harder to hear, until, eventually, the noise was gone.

'I didn't hear it hit anything.'

Delphi stood up and looked to Lyco. He knew what she was thinking straight away. Lyco looked up the hill to the Lighthouse.

'Why would they mark it on the map, but give us this tunnel to escape? It doesn't make sense.'

Right as he spoke, the ground started to rumble.

'Earthquake?' Fera said, her whole body shaking violently.

Lyco tried to steady himself but fell onto the ground. Delphi heard the distinct sound of metal on metal. She looked down the hole, but it still appeared empty.

'Up there!' Fera screamed. They all looked up the hill to the lighthouse. Hundreds upon hundreds of silver balls were bouncing down the street towards them.

'It can't be,' Lyco said in disbelief.

'Start grabbing them!' Fera cried out.

'At that speed, they'll break your fingers!' Lyco said, over the noise.

'Get under cover!' Delphi said, grabbing Fera by the arm.

Lyco followed the girls until they were off the road. The balls were streaming down the street like a wave of metal marbles. They would hit the side gutter and begin to bounce and shoot off in every direction. One flew over their heads and smashed a window on the second floor.

'We have to get out of here!'

'Look, they're heading for the hole!'

As the first few spheres rolled into the hole, they reached the hole and were swallowed in an instant.

'We have to get some of them…we're starving, Delphi!' Fera said, over the loud clattering of the balls.

A scream was heard over the stampeding spheres, but it came from further up the hilly street, closer to the lighthouse.

'Did you hear that?'

Lyco tried to look up, towards the lighthouse, but several balls clanged off the guttering and struck him. One across his arm and one on his head. He stumbled back, blood dripping from his face.

'I'm okay,' he said, sheepishly, knowing he had been standing too close.

'It sounded like a scream, from far up there,' Fera said, pointing.

'We'll head up there, as quickly as we can. Surely this can't last much longer.'

The balls skidded across the road, thousands of them now. They were all skimming the asphalt and making small yellow sparks as they bounced against one another. Halfway up the street, they noticed the balls starting to thin out.

'I think it's over. We have to start collecting them!'

They reached a small shop that had SOAP written on the window. They tried the door, but it was locked. It had an awning that had been torn by rogue balls spraying up into it. They knelt down behind a bin the best they could.

'I'm going out there to see if it can get one,' Delphi said. Lyco grabbed her shirt from behind.

'No way, Delphi,' he said. 'I got hit in the head and it almost knocked me out.'

'But we're up higher now. They don't have a chance to gain so much momentum. It'll be easier.' She pulled away and ran towards the tumbling balls.

They were still rolling moderately fast and snatching them was difficult. One hit her ankle and she leapt up in pain, screaming.

'Delph!' Fera reacted. She ran towards her, reaching down and scooping up two balls that had got stuck in an empty garden plot. She grabbed Delphi and pulled her back.

Lyco saw them heading back towards him and stepped around the metal bin and helped pull them to safety. He glanced up at the top of the street and could see several large containers, all tipped on their side. They were suddenly pulled back on their feet and were being yanked to the left, out of sight.

'I think they're done,' he said, as Delphi and Fera reached him.

From the foray came the sound of hurried voices and yelping.

'Somethings going on up there.'

'Something must have gone wrong?'

Delphi, as fast as her aching ankle would allow her, started up the hill. There was shouting and the slamming of doors. All of a sudden, they could hear the sound of a motor starting. The large black bins were dragged away, leaving a scattering of balls in its wake, tumbling down the steep slope. As they reached the top, they could see the exhaust smoke from a truck disappearing into the packed woodland. Fera let out a small shriek.

'What?' Delphi said. 'What is it?'

Fera was pointing to something several feet away. Lying on the ground, dressed in silver overalls, and wearing a contamination mask, was a person.

Chapter Eight: Knots

'I think he's still alive,' Lyco said, feeling for a pulse.

Delphi removed the mask, somewhat apprehensively. It was a young man. He had barely any stubble. Sandy, unkempt hair flopped over his eyebrows. Lyco inspected him for any breaks or lesions.

'He may have just gotten in the way of the containers when they were tipping out the balls.'

Delphi looked around, expecting someone, or some*thing* to come and retrieve him, but there was no sign of anyone.

'He'll have answers,' Fera said, looking down at the boy with a sideways glance.

'What do you mean?' Lyco said, standing up. His face was a grimace.

'Why we're here? What we're meant to do. He'll know.'

'I highly doubt he will just give over this information.'

'Let's get him off the street first,' Delphi said. 'If they come back, they may use force.'

Lyco and Fera both agreed. Lyco picked him up under his arms while Delphi took the legs. They staggered into the nearest shop and plonked him on a table. It was a butcher's shop with no meat. The display fridges were empty, but the chalk board displayed signs for pork sausages, lamb chops and prime cuts. The boy moaned and moved suddenly. The trio leapt back, trying to find something for a weapon. He kept his eyes shut and tried to roll onto his side. Delphi stepped closer and watched his eyes for movement.

'I think he's still unconscious?'

'We have to tie him up,' Fera said, rummaging through drawers.

'I don't feel great about this idea,' Lyco said. 'It doesn't feel right.'

Delphi helped Fera look for something to tie him up with. 'Lyco,' she said, 'this whole entrapment is against our will. *That* doesn't feel right. We won't hurt him. We just want answers.'

Lyco nodded. He understood what they were saying, but just because they did it, doesn't make it right. He was outnumbered, two to one. He ran to the rear of the store, looking through every cabinet and drawer as he went. Finally, he swung the large fridge door open and rushed inside. It smelt of cleaning fluid and the raw smell of meat permeated through the walls. On a metal shelving unit towards the end of the freezer was a blender. He picked it up to inspect it.

'That might do,' he said, heading back to the main room.

Fera was staring at the boy as if she knew him from somewhere.

'What do you plan on doing with that?' she said, seeing Lyco emerge from the rear of the store.

'I'm going to use the power lead to tie his hands together. Now help me roll him over.'

Fera pushed against the boy's back. He moaned and snored as Lyco quickly tied him up. Right as he was in the middle of his second knot, the boy woke in a panic.

'What the hell?' he gasped, trying to get to his feet. 'What's going on!'

'Stop!' Lyco yelled. 'We found you on the road. We mean you no harm.'

Fera was terrified. Her back was pressed against the display fridge glass.

'Why am I tied up!' the boy screamed, losing balance, and rolling over to his right side. 'Let me go!'

Delphi appeared from the rear office room holding a letter opener. She held it out so the boy could see it.

'Not until you answer questions,' she said. Her voice was

lowered and without reason to think she was joking.

The boy looked at her, then to Fera and then Lyco.

'This shouldn't have happened,' he said, wiggling his body to sit up. His hands were tied tightly behind his back and every time he moved, he winced. 'I'm gonna be in big trouble for this.'

'By who?' Delphi said, taking a step forward.

The boy looked at them all in turn again, then started to laugh.

'What's so funny?'

'You know,' the boy started. 'You hear about the groups, and you see them from a distance… but you never really see them up close, let alone talk to them.'

'Groups?' Lyco mimicked.

'Tell us everything you know… and start from the very beginning.'

'I can't,' he replied. 'I don't have the memories to share.'

'You're one of us?'

'No,' he said. 'I work for them. Someone. I don't know who they are. Instead of payment, I get a memory back. I find out about my life and where I live. It's complicated.'

'So, you *are* one of us,' Fera added.

He grinned again. 'I work here, that's it. I go home to a cubicle and just sleep and eat and then I'm pushed out here to help. I know my job was to push the crates of balls out and then walk around the rear of them and press the controller to lever them up and release them.'

'Simple enough.'

'What went wrong?'

'Mine got jammed. The hydraulic system they use is old. Everything else underground is like new, but they use old stuff aboveground.'

'Underground?' Lyco said, stepping towards him.

'You know, once they do a head count and realise, I'm gone… they'll try find me.'

'How will they find you?'

The boy nodded to the streetlights outside. 'They watch.'

'Wait, stop. We are jumping all over the place... explain what you mean by underground?'

The boy looked at Lyco, as if he were trying to transfer information directly into his brain.

'Every time you drop a ball in a slot, you get a prize. It comes from the underground.'

'Yeah, they give us what we need,' Fera interjected.

'Sometimes,' the boy looked over to her. 'And sometimes what you *don't* need. Depends how you're playing this out.'

'What's the point of all this?'

Boy struggled with his tied hands and started to breath heavily. 'You got to make these looser, it's cutting into my hands.'

'I'll do it,' Fera volunteered.

'No,' Lyco added, stepping in front of her. 'They aren't that tight. I tied them myself.'

Delphi took another step forward, her semi-blunt letter-opener knife still in her hand.

'What's the point of all this?' she repeated, her patience wearing thin.

'My name is Joel,' the boy said. 'Do you know your name? No. I'm seventeen years old... how old are you? You don't know, do you?'

'I know my name. We all do, they were in our pockets when we woke up,' Delphi pulled hers out and waved it in front of his face.

Joel started to laugh again. 'Those aren't your names.'

'What are they then?'

'They're like code names, or nicknames to keep you in groups so the organisers can keep track of where you came from and which group you started in.'

'How do we get out of here?'

Suddenly, a foghorn roared over the small town. It was so loud it made the windows rattle.

'Here they come,' Joel said. 'There's a good chance by the end of the day I won't know my name either.'

'How are they doing this?'

'Look,' Joel said, his voice sounded profoundly serious. 'If you want to stay hidden, let me go. I'll tell you something that will help you… trust me.'

'No way,' Lyco snapped.

'I'm willing to do it,' Fera said, turning to Delphi.

'We can't trust you,' Delphi said, lowering the knife. 'But we don't really have a choice.'

'Delphi,' Lyco argued. 'We do have a choice… we can use him against them. Hold him hostage until they let us go.'

Delphi looked at Lyco. 'You heard him… he knows his name and age and that's all. He's a player in this game too… like us.'

She walked over to him and untied the knots. Joel leapt to his feet and ran to the door. He pushed against the glass and looked back, over his shoulder.

'There's an old cottage in the woods. It's fairly hidden. Follow the last road east. You'll find answers in there,' he pushed the door all the way opened and ran out into the street.

They all stood there in stunned silence for a few moments.

'We should get out of here too. There's a rear exit. We'll find somewhere where they can't see us,' Delphi instructed.

Fera and Lyco agreed and followed her out of the butcher's shop.

Chapter Nine: Rebellious

The sun had dipped quickly, and they had agreed not to be out in the streets at night. They took refuge in an old church down a side road. Together they had pooled their ball collection and had three silver balls and one that seemed to gleam like oil. In the right light, it looked almost purple.

'I was trying to grab them as they were being flung at me,' Lyco said, still nursing a sore head.

Delphi had taken one of the silver spheres and found a chute. Inside she got firewood, kindling, and a small fire starter kit. Lyco had found a black metal fire pit leaning outside the neighbour's house. He had dragged it inside and set it up in the centre of the room. The pews were pushed to the side. The church's high ceilings and dusty floor gave everyone an eerie feeling. At the end of the room was a small stage area with a priest's podium. Spider webs hung from the lectern onto the floor. Several dead flies were stuck in the web, long dead and drained of their bodily fluids.

Delphi had the purple, oily sphere in her hand, rotating it around and around with her fingers, watching as the reflection of the flames stayed in the same area. Lyco lay on his back, staring up the ceiling.

'This cottage in the woods,' he said. 'Surely, we are not going to that first. I think finding the 'X' on the map is our first stop tomorrow.'

Delphi didn't say anything for a few seconds. 'If the 'X' is our final destination,' she said looking over the licking flames, towards Lyco. 'I think we will need to look at the cottage first.'

Fera sat with her knees up to her chest. Her arms were

wrapped around her shins. She was rocking back and forth, trying to keep warm. Her gaze was set on the fire.

'I'm hungry,' she finally blurted.

Delphi stood up. She slipped the purple sphere into her pocket.

'I'll use one of the balls and hopefully get us food.'

'Don't you think we should save them?' Lyco said, not taking his tired eyes off the ceiling.

'For what?' Fera asked.

'If we get inside the lighthouse, we might need it to get weapons or something to help us.'

'If I use one, we have two more, plus, we won't be any use if we are starving.'

Lyco didn't say anymore.

'I'll go with you,' Fera said.

'I'll be fine. Stay here and warm yourself. I won't be long.'

'Are you sure?' Lyco said, his voice sounded extremely sleepy.

'I'll be back before you know it.'

'Maybe just use one ball. The silver one,' Lyco said. 'Hopefully, it will give us some food or something else we might need.'

Delphi headed to the rear of the church and into a small hallway. It was barely lit by the fire. She could hear Fera and Lyco talking, but she couldn't make out what they were saying. She went through a small room and out a rear door. The fur coat was keeping her warm.

Two houses down Delphi found an empty pet store. The front window had an advertisement painted on it for tropical fish and rabbit food. The paint had started to peel away. She pushed on the door and slipped inside. Lining the walls were empty fish tanks and cages. On the floor were multiple bags of seed, all full and unopened. As she walked through to the back rooms, she could still smell the animals. All the cage doors were open. On the floor, in the surgery room was a hole. A chute door was on the wall to her left. She pulled out one silver ball and the plum-coloured ball and looked at both.

She knew the other two were expecting her to use the silver ball, as it had given them what they wanted last time. Her dark outline reflected in the oily sphere. *Maybe this will give us something we need if the game continues?* She thought. *Maybe it will give us food and a way out of here?* She plunged the purple ball down the hole and listened. She could hear it scrape and drop along chains and slide down metal pipes. Cogs and gears moved and then it went quiet. Suddenly there was a loud *pop* from outside. She looked up and ran out the front door and onto the street. Far on the hill, the light house started to make strange noises. It sounded like it was about to tear away from its foundations and fly skyward. She stepped back, even though she was far away from it. It creaked and moaned and then, finally, its light came on. The beacon was pure white light and shone straight into the middle of town. Its perfect line of light shone over her head in a dazzling beam. She looked up at it in awe. On the road, ahead of her, she could see Lyco and Fera both run out into the street.

'Delphi? Are you okay?' Fera said, running to her.

'How did you do that?' Lyco said, his mouth agape.

'I used the…' she hesitated, hoping they wouldn't get mad at her. 'Purple ball.'

Fera smiled, as did Lyco. 'What do you think it means?' he said.

'It's looking towards the fountain we saw.'

'Wait, it's starting to move,' Lyco said, pointing up at the lighthouse.

The light starting to spin around, slowly. Delphi pulled out another silver ball and held it up to the light. 'Let's hope for food this time.'

No one said anything as she disappeared inside. Lyco took his eyes away from the light and looked at Fera. 'Can you smell…the ocean?'

Fera sniffed the air. 'I think so? I don't remember the ocean… but it is the first thing that comes to mind when I smell it.'

They stood in the middle of the street and looked around for any explanation for the strange new smell.

'Hope you like tuna,' Delphi said, appearing behind them. She had a loaf of bread, butter, and a large can of tuna.

They returned to the church and sat around the burning embers and ate tuna out of a can. Fera spread the butter thick on her slice of bread and was eating it with pleasure. Lyco had eaten a tuna sandwich and was lying back contemplating another one. Delphi was examining the can in the firelight.

'They've scratched off the expiry date,' she said.

Lyco looked over to her. 'Why would they do that?'

'So, we don't know what year it is,' Fera replied, reaching for another slice of bread. The bread packet was crinkled butchers' paper with no discernible markings on it.

'When we get out of here, I'm going to ask them why it was so important that we couldn't remember who we were or what year it is.'

'Seems like they want to watch how we work together, as a group of strangers. Maybe that's how it ends? We work out who we are?'

'If they wanted to watch us work together, they could do that without erasing our memory,' Fera added, biting into her bread.

'Maybe they think people's pasts effect how they react in situations, or how they interact with people.'

'Maybe it's punishment?' Delphi said, laying back, her belly full.

'Either way, it's morbid.'

'Hopefully, the lighthouse, or the cabin will provide some answers.'

After an hour of eating and getting comfortable, all three finally started to sleep. The glow from the fire filled the old church. It cast long shadows onto the walls as the fire crackled and provided warmth. The ground was hard and cold, but after a few hours the small church filled with warmth. The stained-glass windows reflected the dancing flames.

Fera suddenly woke in fright as the front doors were smashed inwards. Delphi opened her eyes and looked up at the ceiling. She thought the room was caving in. A long metal claw flew in through the front door, attached to a long, polished silver chain. It clattered on the ground like a hungry animal. Lyco turned, his face stricken with fear as the clamp leapt from the ground and clamped itself around him. He tried to stand up but was reefed to the ground.

'Help!' He screamed in fright, as the strength of it jerked him backwards and onto his backside, dragging him towards the door.

'Lyco!' Delphi screamed, running towards him.

Broken pieces of door were scattered in front of the main entrance. Fera bolted towards Lyco and reached out, gripping his fingers. The chains jerked him with extreme power, launching him through the air and out into the darkened street. The clamp around Lyco looked like a metal hand. Silver fingers gripped his waist. They had moving cogs for knuckles and sliding pistons for finger joints. Delphi bolted towards him, jumping over the detritus and diving for him. A van was facing the opposite way with its rear doors open. Several dark figures were operating a machine that fed the chain. Delphi turned her attention away from Lyco and ran towards the van.

'Let him go!' she screamed. Her voice hoarse.

Lyco, panicking, pushed down on the clamp, but it became tighter. He started to be gripped so hard his lungs were gasping for breath. Fera was only small, compared to Lyco, but she was pulling his arms out of the metal hands' grip. Lyco wiggled as much as he could, slowly feeling himself becoming free of the bind. The chain yanked again, and he was thrown to the ground, smashing his shoulder and elbow on the hard asphalt. He gasped in pain and held his arm as he was dragged on his back towards the vans opened doors. Delphi was close to it when the occupants started the engine and the van roared to life. Bright floodlights beamed across the road, illuminating Delphi.

'Stand back, don't make us shoot you,' said a strange robotic voice.

Her eyes stung from the lights. She covered them with her hand. 'Let him go!'

One of the hooded figures stepped forward. It was cast in silhouette.

'We're taking him, Delphi,' said a man's voice. It was calm and steady. 'Don't make this harder than it already is.'

Delphi stopped moving forward and stood her ground. Lyco slowly got to his feet. His arm bleeding and his shoulder looked dislocated. Fera ran to Lyco, tears in her eyes as she pulled at the clamp, trying to tear it from him.

'Fera,' Delphi said, keeping her eyes on the shadowy man in front of her. 'Stop.'

'They can't take him!' she cried desperately. 'They can't take him, Delph!'

'Fera,' Delphi roared. She was calm but knew when these people were going to take something, they took it. 'Stop. Lyco is gone.'

The chain slowly moved towards the van as a mob of disguised soldiers moved towards Lyco and tossed a hessian sack over his head, dragging him into the van. The van skidded through the dark, shutting off its floodlights and leaving Delphi and Fera alone in the middle of the street.

Chapter Ten: Too Many Questions and No Answers

Follow the last road east, Delphi said in her mind. She kept repeating it as Fera drank from the water bottle. The fire was nothing but small glowing embers. The morning sun had come through the stained-glass windows, making the church dance in an array of colours.

Delphi studied the map. She turned it and turned it again.

'What are you looking for?' Fera finally asked, extinguishing the last of the smouldering ash.

'The last road east. I never bothered to learn where north was… until this morning,' She pointed to the map. 'This is the last road that goes east. It's right before the lighthouse.'

Fera squatted next to her. 'Are you sure you want to go there first?'

'The boy…Joel, said we could get answers there.'

'But wouldn't you just want to leave? Whatever is up there will have answers too,' Fera protested.

'I'm not asking you to come, Fera. If you want to head up into the lighthouse, I will meet you there.' Delphi stood up and stretched her back and arms. Her clothes were dirty, and she could feel a thin film of ash on her face.

They headed for the door and out into the warm morning sun. Fera knew she would go wherever Delphi went. She didn't want to be separated again.

They walked up the road and passed more empty stores. There were several streets with houses, all sitting quiet and presumably empty. Once they reached the peak of the hill, they could see the lighthouse in all its glory. It looked magnificent with its red and white striped body and huge light cage sitting on top of it like a crown. Around the bottom were large stones covered in moss and grass growing out between them. Delphi could see a freshly painted wooden door. She knew it was painted recently as it didn't have the weather scarring that the rest of the lighthouse had. Fera looked right and left. Both lanes of road lead to a jumble of houses.

'Which way?'

Delphi pointed to the right. 'As long as the sun rises and sets the same here, this should be east.'

Fera took the lead and started the trek through the rows of identical houses. She could smell the sea but couldn't see it through the stacked buildings.

'What do you think happened to Lyco?'

'I don't know?' Delphi replied, her voice sullen. 'If this is a game, maybe he lost somehow?'

'By doing what?' Fera asked, looking over to her.

Delphi shrugged. 'Who knows? Maybe they choose at random? Maybe we dropped the wrong colour ball into a chute? Hopefully, this place we are going to will tell us.'

Fera continued walking. She didn't want to speak anymore as there were too many questions and no answers. They walked along the side of the road in the shade until they reached the very end of the road. It didn't fade into grass, or have a fence, it merely just stopped. There was a line where the asphalt was, then it was long, wavering grass.

Fera stood with the grass gently brushing against her shin and her prosthetic leg. 'Now what?'

'Up there,' Delphi pointed. Through the brush and pine trees choking the border, a small red brick chimney could be seen.

Fera looked at Delphi and they both nodded to each other in agreement to head that way. There was no clear path through the grassy allotment, so they went straight through the long grass, towards the boundary of trees. The grass was getting longer and longer until it was up to their hips.

Delphi turned to look for Fera who had fallen a few meters behind her.

'Stick by me, Fera.'

Fera looked down just in time to see something slither out of view.

'Delph,' she said, the word shaking with fear. 'I think something is in here.'

Delphi looked down and could see a curled up, brown snake with a red underbelly looking up at her.

'Don't move.'

'Delphi...' fear crept into Fera's voice. 'It's sliding up my leg.'

Delphi went to move, but noticed she was surrounded by snakes hidden in the long grass. The entire ground was covered. A rippling motion went over the grass like a wave of scales.

'Fera, stop moving,' Delphi commanded, seeing that Fera had started to step back. She could see that Fera was on the edge of panic. 'Fera, listen to my voice.'

'Delphi, there are so many!'

One small green snake leapt forward and bit Fera on the metal shin. It let go immediately. Although her leg was prosthetic, Fera could still feel its strike. Another one suddenly sunk its fangs into the flesh of her other leg. She screamed and went to step away, but stood on a huge, six-foot-long python. She lost her balance from the quick succession of bites and fell back into the scaly pit. As she hit the ground, she felt her skin touch the snake's smooth flesh. She howled in horror and thrashed her body around, trying to get them to stop crawling onto her. One sunk its fangs into her abdomen, then another. A long snake with a diamond head lashed out, biting her on the face. She felt a hand reach down into the grass and yank her to her feet. It was Delphi. She was standing there, holding a snake around its head to stop it from biting her. Delphi stomped her foot down on another snake's head to stop it from slithering onto Fera.

'This way,' Delphi said, trying to keep her cool. She dragged Fera behind her.

They ran to the left, out of the thickest part of the grassy field and along a dirty ridge until they reached the line of trees. Fera stumbled and fell. Her face looked pale and sickly. She lifted her shirt and exposed several snake bites.

'What if they're poisonous?' she said, looking up to Delphi.

Delphi looked around and could see the cabin through the tangle of forestry. She looked back at Fera who started to close her eyes.

'Fera, stay awake. Stay with me,' she got Fera to her feet and wrapped her arms around her and steadily walked towards the cabin. 'There may be anti-venom or something in there.'

The climb was arduous, and each step was getting more and more difficult. Delphi could feel Fera's ability to walk starting to slow.

'Stay with me, Fera,' Delphi said, pleading. 'Help!' she screamed as the cabin got into view. 'Someone…please! Help!'

She lay Fera down on the ground just outside the cabin. It appeared to be built out of trees cleared from around the area. Horizontal slats of huge pines made the walls and criss-crossed hatched sticks created a domed roof. The chimney was the only brick element to the whole house. To the rear of the roof was several antennae and wires prodding the air. Delphi ran up the stairs to the balcony and rattled on the door with her fist. She could feel her energy sapping from her bites.

'Help us please! We don't want to play anymore. Please help!'

The door opened. A man with a white face mask wearing headphones stood there. Two holes were cut out of the fabric for his eyes. He looked in utter shock.

'Please…don't hurt me… I just…'

'Please help us,' Delphi stepped up to him. 'We've been bitten by snakes in the field.'

The man, who had a microphone attached to his headset, slid it off. 'You shouldn't be here… they'll be angry.'

Delphi clutched him by his shirt. 'Help us!' She suddenly felt weak in the knees and fell forward. The man caught her under the arms and lay her down in the doorway. He stepped back and slung his headphone mic back on. Delphi saw swirls of black in her vision and every joint started to ach and throb with intense pain. She tried to open her eyes, but then there was a painful stabbing sensation in her stomach. When she peeled one eye open again, she was being dragged inside and lifted onto a couch.

'Fera,' she managed to whisper. Her voice was groggy, and her body felt like it was filled with cotton wool.

When she opened her eyes again, the whole ceiling was warping and spinning. She tried to sit up, but her head was doing somersaults. Slowly, she moved off the couch and tried to stand, but her whole body felt like it was on fire. She got down on her hands and knees and headed to the door. Gingerly, she started to pull herself up on the doorframe. She looked past the balcony and could see someone attending to Fera. They were wearing a pure white outfit, their face covered like the man who greeted her at the cabin doorway, except they had a red cross printed on their back. They were also wearing a mask and gloves.

Fera was placed on a stretcher and lifted by four others with the same red cross.

'Fera!' Delphi called out, suddenly losing her balance, and tripping backwards. She lay on the ground and looked up at the ceiling, slowly the darkness crept in, and she blacked out.

Chapter Eleven: Pure Black

When Delphi woke, she was alone. She was slumped against the front door. The pain in her stomach had subsided, but it was still a dull ache. The trees were gently swaying in an easterly breeze. She could feel it on her face. The snake bites on her shins were swollen and felt cold in the breeze. She still felt groggy and looked over to where Fera had collapsed. She was gone. Delphi reached up to the door handle and got to her feet. Her knees were weak, and her stance was shaky. On the ground next to her was a vial and a needle in a packet. She picked it up and tried to read it, but her vision was still blurry. She shook her head and tried to focus. On the vial were the words *anti-venom*. The bottle had not been pierced and the needle clearly hadn't been used. She turned away from the door and strode over to the couch. It was the same couch in every house she had been in. In fact, the house was furnished much like the houses along every street, except for the far-left corner. There was a table with several monitors, a radio transmitter, and several books. She picked up the vial and syringe and slowly made her way over to the table and slumped down on the chair. She carefully placed the anti-venom kit beside her. Her eyes were trying to focus but kept crossing images. She shook her head and looked at the monitor. It was separated into four smaller screens, each one showing different areas of the town. The first one was showing the entrance to the town, where they had come in, now days ago. The second one was the water fountain. There appeared to be some people gathered around it, all wearing protective gear. They were pouring something into the water.

The third showed the large department store, Norway's and the last one was the exterior of the church.

'These are all places I've been to,' Delphi said, still feeling nauseous.

Her head was swimming and foggy and she looked down at the anti-venom. The snake attack was still fresh in her mind, but she wasn't sure what was real or not anymore. *They felt real and the effects seemed to be real, but why would they leave me here? They took Fera*, she thought, *but not me.*

In front of her lay the books. They looked like logbooks, or notebooks of some kind. She started to flip through them, even though she could barely make out the words. There were times for things, arrival dates with no year. She skipped a few pages and found a rough sketch of a machine. It housed three large cylinders. It looked like a crude drawing of the one they used to drop the balls down the street. Her hands went to her pockets to see if she still had any spheres, but they were gone. She couldn't remember if she had any left, or if they had been taken. Her mind suddenly did a backflip and she slipped onto the ground. Everything around her went fuzzy. Slowly, she reached up to the bottle and the syringe and pulled it down. Her stomach was cramping again, and she felt close to blacking out but she managed to fill the syringe and inject herself with the clear solution. As she fell back down onto the cold ground, she could see several twin bite marks up her leg and arm. They were all red and aggravated.

By the time she woke up, it was night. The house was dark, and air was still and cold. She sat up, feeling hungry, but with a nearly clear mind. She sat at the desk and rifled through the books. On the very bottom of the pile was a book in a green leather case. She opened it to reveal several paragraphs of handwritten notes.

Group 8862 – This group has been plagued with disaster from the very start. The reptiles were not fed properly and attacked them. I have made a complaint to the Regulators. The serpents are lacking the correct de-fanging procedure and the venom is still toxic.

Delphi read further.

The air marshal called to discuss the lighthouse. New bulbs have been fitted. If the trigger is activated, the light will shine the way. They will not be dropping supplies once the light is on.

We are on Sight duty for the length of this process. If it takes them weeks to get through to the lighthouse, we could be on rations. It should not take them too long as they seem to be getting through the traps quicker than the last group.

Sitting here, I can't help but become disgruntled with the last group. This does not seem to be worth the pittance in pay. A memory here and a day of freedom there. I feel like rushing into the middle of the town square and decrying my allegiance to the Apostasy. But, I fear, like many others, that my brain will be wiped, and I'll be the next 'contestant' to enter this maze of mayhem and murder.

Delphi sat back in her chair. *I am in a game after all.* She heard the familiar sound of a ball falling in the ceiling and leapt to her feet. It was a sound she was most familiar with, it felt right.

Clank!

It rolled around the roof, falling in between rails and down holes until it fell into a wall and started to slide away from her. Delphi ran. Her fingertips running along the wall, following it. Toward the end of the hallway, the orb rolled into the next room where there was a spout. It shot out, fast and bounced along the ground, heading for a depression in the room that ended in a hole. Delphi took two quick steps and snatched it on the third bounce. It was pure black. She knew she hadn't seen any other like it, not that she could remember. She slipped it back into her pocket and quickly checked the remainder of the house. One room had a proper bed, with sheets that were dirty and tossed haphazardly over the mattress. Beside it, on the bedside table was a notepad and pen. The notepad had nearly every page ripped out of it. There was a clock, which was either broken, or just displayed the same time, *11:11*. There was a pair of shoes under the bed. They were more like boots, with an athletic sole. She tried them on, but they were far too big. In the next room was a made bed. It had exactly the same bedside table, but the clock read *12:12*. On the wall, was the outline of a chute. A small hole was above it, staring at her like an inky eye. Delphi walked up to it and stared into it. It was tempting to slide the ball inside, but something inside her told her not to. The temptation may be great, but what if nothing happened? What if it just gave her firewood or a shovel? She patted the ball in her pocket and left the room.

Once she got to the lounge room, she could smell smoke. It was smoke from a fire close by. She looked around quickly, then ran outside. Down the forest trail and into the town, she could see one of the houses on fire. The flames were licking the sky, sending black plumes bellowing into the night. She bolted through the dark, without a care for any lingering snakes and ran down the path. The thick smell of timber burning filled her nostrils as she reached the road. As she approached the flaming house, she could feel the heat radiate off it like waves of volcanic waste. She swung her arm up to protect herself from the blaring hot glare. Ash was falling like rain down on her. From deep inside the inferno, she could hear a voice.

'Help! Delphi, help!'

'Fera?' Delphi screeched.

She ran to the front steps, which were flanked in fire and made her way to the door. She noticed the doorknob was pulsating with red hot heat, so she kicked at it as hard as she could. The door buckled inwards, and a burst of flames erupted from the inside. It scorched her hands and clothing. She took a few steps backward, trying to gather herself.

'Delphi, help me!' came the voice again over the roaring fire.

She bent down to try and look through the smoke but could only see patches of fire on the ground and the couch turning to glowing coals. The walls were coated in flickering flames. She took a deep breath and ran inside. Her shirt caught fire instantly, as did her left pant leg. She ran as fast as she could, the smoke burning her eyes and feet. She searched the front room, but could only see the table, chairs and fireplace.

'Fera!'

'Delphi, help!'

The reply came from one of the back rooms. She bolted down the hallway. On either side, long flames licked at her hair. She could feel blisters bulging under her feet. She lent forwards and ran. She could smell her hair singing.

'Fera!'

She searched the first room. It was almost entirely engulfed in fire. She ran to the second room.

'Delphi help!' said a loud voice.

'Fera!' Delphi replied, hearing the voice from within the room.

Her feet started to burn as she searched the room for Fera. Her loud screaming was coming from under the bed.

'Fera?' she said, risking her knees getting burnt by getting to the floor and looking under the bed. She reached in and pulled out a large speaker. In the back was a cassette tape. It was halfway through its reel.

'Delphi! Help!' the speaker screamed.

Suddenly from above came the crashing noise of the ceiling collapsing. Delphi leapt out of the way as a beam came through the plaster ceiling, landing at her feet. It sent sparks and embers flying across the room. She threw the speaker into the fire and ran back down the hallway. The entire house was now engulfed in smoke. She got as close to the floor as she could, but still could barely breathe. Her feet were now bleeding and sore. As she got to the door, she noticed it was closed. Someone had put a new door in the frame! She reached up, burning her hands as she turned it. She screamed in agony and as the door peeled open, the draft sent the smoke bellowing out into the night sky. She crawled along the balcony, coughing, and spitting until she reached the lawn and rolled onto her back. Standing all around her, were figures cloaked in hoods.

'Your time has come to an end, Delphi.'

Chapter Twelve: Spirited Away

Delphi looked up at the night sky. She could see the pluming smoke going higher and higher into the starry night. Then it appeared to hit something and gather like a thunder cloud. *The stars aren't real,* she thought, *but they are still beautiful.*

'You didn't make it,' said a voice. 'It's time to stop running. Stop fighting. It's time to stop.' The voice was trying to be commanding, but it was failing miserably.

Delphi sat up and shook the grass and ash out of her hair. Her feet hurt and her arm was bleeding. She could still feel the black orb in her pocket. She turned to the road and could see two vans parked facing each other. Several robed people stood in front of them, with their faces covered in masks. Their long cloaks went to their ankles, but their thick, black boots and high woollen socks could still be seen.

'Didn't make it to what?' she asked, getting to her feet.

'This is the end. It's time to come with us.'

'Come home,' said another voice. The first hooded creature turned and looked at the person who had just spoke, as if they were surprised, they had said it.

'Home? I don't think you'll take me home,' Delphi said, smiling, stepping slowly back towards the burning house. 'I think if you get me to go with you, they will give you a memory back… maybe a day of freedom. Sounds good to me, but I going to fight you. I will not play this game any longer.'

'You've paid your penance. It's time to give up,' the voice was of a man. It came from the rear of the group. Delphi guessed him to be young. She thought maybe this was his first time doing this.

'You know,' Delphi said, nonchalantly putting one foot on

the steps, 'I'm starting to remember.'

'Impossible.'

'Is it?' Delphi said. 'I've been out here for a while. Maybe whatever you are giving me is starting to wear off. Maybe the anti-venom played havoc with the chemicals you gave me to forget who I am?'

Overhead, she could hear the whooping of a helicopter. One was coming from the east and one from the west.

'Delphi, we don't want you to harm yourself anymore. You need medical help. If your memories are returning, like you say they are, then you would remember the agreement.'

Delphi smiled, then started to laugh.

'It's a little hazy,' she said, and turned and bolted back into the inferno.

'Get her!'

Several of the cloaked figures bolted towards her, chasing her over the threshold of the house. A beam came tumbling down through the ceiling plaster, taking out one of the chasers. Another one caught fire from the spitting flames and ran towards the window, throwing themselves through it while screaming in terror. A loud siren could be heard rushing down the street as Delphi made her way into one of the rear rooms. On the wall was a hole and a chute. She yanked the ball from her pocket and looked at it. It reflected the raging fire burning all around her.

'Stop!' came the scream from behind her.

She turned to see who it was and ducked just with a second to spare as a firefighter's axe was brought down towards her head. It stuck into the wall with a sickening thud. Delphi instinctively kicked out at the attacker. Its long coat catching fire as it went toppling backwards. She turned, snatched the axe from the wall and jammed the ball into the hole. There came a sound of loud screeching followed by grinding gears and stiff cogs. The chute spat open, and Delphi climbed into it, closing it behind her.

There was a moment of utter silence. Delphi sat on

something that felt metal, then came the pounding of fists on the chute door behind her. Whatever she was sitting on tilted forward and she started to slide. She lay down and held the axe over her chest. She was moving fast down a slide but couldn't see anything. It felt like she was being spirited away by some unknown force. Cold air slid over her face and cooled her blistered skin. She could smell her burnt hair and her feet throbbed.

Suddenly, the small chamber she was in opened and she could see the underbelly of the road and houses above her. Plumbing pipes and cables hung like bats from the dirt and metal ceiling. All around her were small balls moving along conveyer belts, heading in every direction. Mechanical stairs churned trees in pots and pieces of houses up, towards the ceiling. Trap doors opened and closed, and small bundles of rope and shovels were being taken along tracks in small buckets. Everything was copasetic.

She felt a sudden drop as she was flung towards an open tube. She braced for impact but had been scooped up in a metal bin and elevated upward. She peered over the ledge and could see several workers down below pointing towards her. She looked up, seeing several doors and chute openings. People in masks were loading the chutes. They all froze to stare at her.

She stood up and leapt out of the swaying bucket, swinging her axe over her head, and catching it on another chain that brought her up to a door frame with a concrete lip. She pushed through it and out the other side. She collapsed on soft carpet and quickly got to her feet. She held the axe in an attack position, ready to strike, but there was no one there. Her breath was quick and gasping until she realised, she was alone in a house.

She lowered the axe and peered out the doorway and into the hall. It was one of the cloned houses. Slowly, she tiptoed out into the lounge. The lounge she had seen over and over again, except this one wasn't on fire. She moved to the window and pulled the curtain across. She appeared to be at the end of the road, right next to the lighthouse. As she moved to the front door, she could hear an alarm going off in the distance.

They know I've escaped, she said to herself.

She flung the front door open and bolted towards the lighthouse. Stones lined a dying garden that dotted the pathway up to the front door. It was getting dark as the flood lights from the car had been turned off and the burning house had been extinguished. She knew all too well now that they had cameras everywhere and had been watching their every move. Whoever *they* were.

From far behind her came the heavy pounding of footsteps. Doors and chutes from every house around her suddenly burst open with robed, masked figures, all brandishing weapons and rope. She reached the door of the lighthouse and twisted the old, iron handle, but it was locked. She swung the axe back and brought it down hard on the door. A large, lightning bolt shaped scar shot down the wood. She yanked it out and tried again, tearing half the door away. It fell to the ground in pieces.

'There she is!' she could hear them screaming from the bottom of the road.

She crawled in through the gaping hole in the door. The bottom level was circular concrete with the white stairs ascending clockwise up the lighthouse. Her thighs and calf muscles burnt, but she pushed on through the pain. As she rounded the first bend, she could hear the door behind her getting smashed to splinters. They were coming through, fast. Hearing their heavy footfalls made her run even faster. She thought of ditching the axe but thought better of it. It would be lighter, and she could run faster, but it was her only weapon.

As she went around and around, her head began to swim with dizziness. Suddenly the never-ending stairs opened up into what appeared to be a control room. Old dials and pulley levers lined one wall. There was a chair pushed into an old pine desk that had been collecting dust and cobwebs for some time.

'There!' came a voice from behind her.

She swung around to see a faceless figure lunge towards her. She ducked and weaved past him, pushing him to the ground with the axe handle. Another figure had climbed the stairs and reached out to grab her. He had snatched her around her shirt sleeve and tore it off. Delphi screamed and bolted up the stairs. The next level was a bedroom. A single bed lay against the rear wall with a window. The glass was foggy and cracked. There were slippers by the bed and a robe hanging on a hook. She didn't want to stop to check the room, as the staircase was now full of stomping boots. A service room was just around the bend when she tripped on the last step and toppled over, grating her already bruised and injured legs. The axe skidded across the floor and hit the base of an old piece of machinery stacked up against the far corner. An arm reached down and gripped her wrist.

'Stop running,' said a woman's heavy voice. 'You'll just make it worse... trust me.'

Delphi looked through the mask and into her eyes.

'I know you,' she said, wracking her brain for the memory. She looked familiar, but the image and name belonging to her had faded.

'You can't make it, no one does,' the woman said as several more figures pushed past her and clutched Delphi by her arms.

'You don't even know what you're fighting for,' said one of them, at almost a whisper.

They lifted her up into the air and headed back down the stairs.

'If you're trying to stop me, then it must be worth fighting for,' Delphi screamed and squirmed her body, loosening the grip from the left captor. She dropped and turned so she would hit the ground with her shoulder. She kicked out at the remaining figure, sending their knee buckling sideways. She scrambled to her feet and ran to the staircase, flying up it as fast as her body would take her. Her heart beating fast in her chest.

It was two more turns of the stairs until she reached the lantern room. She could see the lantern pane in all its glory. The room seemed larger than it should have been. The rhombus lightbulb was spectacular. She stood in front of it, feeling blood trickle from her arm and shoulder. Under her feet were small puddles of blood from the popped blisters. Slowly, a single person's footsteps started coming up the stairwell. Delphi glanced over her shoulder. She could see a chute along the wall with a ball hole. She tapped her pockets, but she was all out of spheres.

A man walked up the stairs with neat, shortly cut hair and thin wired glasses. He already had a smile on his face.

'Ah, we meet again.'

'I've never met you,' Delphi said, stepping back and pushing her back against the lantern pane railing.

'Oh, but we have,' the man said, pulling a notepad from under his arm. He licked his finger and started flipping through the pages.

'I got to the place on the map,' Delphi said, watching him carefully. 'You have to let me go now… I won.'

The man looked at Delphi over his glasses. His teethy grin sent wrinkled up his stout face.

'Won?' he snapped. 'There is no winner here. But tell me, *Delphi*, you told one of our employees that you were starting to remember… is this true?'

Delphi didn't answer for a moment. She was looking around the room for another escape hatch.

'Maybe.'

The man reached into his jacket and pulled out several polaroid pictures.

'I doubt it's true. No one in ten years has come out of it in the middle of…' he caught his words and his eyes flicked. He was angry at himself for the slip of his tongue. He knew she had caught it too. 'I'll tell you what,' he handed her the polaroids. 'You tell me who these people are, and I'll give you a little hint.'

Reluctantly, Delphi reached forward and took the pictures. She fanned them out.

'This one is Hasse,' she said, holding a picture up of the woman who had been taken in the department store. 'This is Lyco,' she said, looking at the picture of the man. 'He was taken from the church. And this,' tears started to fill her eyes. 'Is Fera. Is she alive?'

The man banged his heels together and stood as straight as his back would allow.

'She is. Is that all you recognise of them?'

'What do you mean?'

The man gingerly walked over and pointed at each one in turn. 'Your mother, your father and your sister.'

Delphi dropped the photos on the ground and let the tears fall from her face. They rolled over her cheeks and dripped off her jawline.

'What is this? Why are you doing this to me?'

'Delphi, we aren't doing it to you… you are doing it to yourself. You are the one that keeps insisting on continuing. I give you a black ball at the end of your first game. Then, at the start of this trial, you give it back.'

The chute door opened, and mint green gas started to pour from the wall. The man slid a facemask over his nostrils and mouth.

'I do enjoy coming to see you at the end of each round though. You're tough. Hopefully, I'll see you again shortly.'

With that the man turned on his heels and headed back down the lighthouse. Delphi gasped for air and fell to her knees. She tried to crawl after him, but all her limbs suddenly lost feeling. A memory of horses arose in her mind, and she fell into a deep sleep.

Acknowledgments

After the first book, there were a lot of questions. I went into this series wanting to hold back as much as I could. My goal was to drip feed the reader tiny morsels of information to keep them guessing. Did this book provide you all the answers? I'm sure it didn't. It did however give you enough to come back for the rest. It's a strange complex story that I thought long and hard about and I'm hoping you will enjoy reading it, as much as I enjoyed writing it.

I would like to thank Sabrina for pushing me forward and giving me inspiration, Jenny for relentlessly hearing about the entire story arc and then editing it with a red pen. My family for your undying support and anyone that comes to the conventions and is interested in my books and spends their hard-earned coin to pick up my stuff, I thank you.

For more information visit
www.ouroborusbooks.com

CPSIA information can be obtained
at www.ICGtesting.com
Printed in the USA
LVHW090745181022
730903LV00015B/713